GAME ON!

R.F. BLACKSTONE

SEVERED PRESS

GAME ON!

WWW.SEVEREDPRESS.COM

ISBN: 978-1-922861-35-1

Also by R.F. Blackstone:

Zombie Nazis On A Train
The Wild Hunt
Megaflora
The Valley Of Bicho
The Book Of Spite
Flicker
Kaiju World
Big Smoke

CHAPTER ONE

Move ya ass!

The thought repeated until it became a driving rhythm that propelled Mark Crowe forward through the low hanging vines, branches and thick, heavy leaves. He knew he couldn't keep going like this forever. Eventually, they would catch up to him and then game over.

Game over, the phrase danced in his head as the death-cries of the others surrounded him. Each one was preceded by a low growl, then the sickening wet crunch of jaws closing around flesh and the shredding of skin and muscle.

He couldn't focus on the horrors; he had to keep moving.

His foot caught on a gnarled root, sending him tumbling to the ground. A gasp of pain escaped his lips as jagged bark sliced his hand open.

Scrambling to his feet, Crowe forced himself to push the pain away and focus on what he had to do. If he could survive for another hour, everything would be okay. That was the deadline, and once reached, he'd be free and with more money than he could ever spend in a lifetime.

But his chances of success lessened with each passing second.

Tearing his soiled shirt, he wrapped the length of cloth around his injured hand and pulled on it hard. He couldn't risk any blood staining the foliage, giving away his position. Satisfied with his make-shift bandage, Mark jammed his hand into the crook of his arm and set off again, weaving his way through the thick tropical jungle.

Even though he hadn't slept in at least two days, his senses were hyped up and working overtime. His nose twitched on its own, taking in every scent it could, ignoring the horrid stench of his own fear mixed with sweat and piss. There was no way his olfactory could match that of an animal, but his job as a chef helped to cultivate his ability to distinguish smells and flavours.

Focus! his mind screamed at him. This wasn't the time to get lost in his own thoughts and memories. He'd seen the others do the same and their fates had been short, painful, and bloody.

Shaking his head, the snap of a branch froze him. Doing his best to hold his shuddering breath, Crowe ignored the pounding of his heart and the rushing of blood in his veins.

Instead, he focused on the sound.

His eyes scanned the area, which was laughable since the moon was hidden behind clouds and he didn't have a flashlight. Squinting into the darkness, Crowe forced his eyes to differentiate between the trees, bushes, shrubs, and anything that was remotely human shaped.

Move! Even though he knew that the longer he stood still, the greater his chances were of being killed, his inherent curiosity was more powerful than his survival instinct.

A small smile crept across his mouth as he thought, *Besides, the worst thing that can happen is death.* The giggle came without warning, as did the crack of a gunshot.

Without realising it, Crowe's feet moved on their own and he was off and running once more. Holding both hands up to protect his face from the trees, vines and any traps set by his captors, he didn't care about the plant life. His childhood had taken care of that with all the camping trips. But the traps? That was a different matter altogether.

He'd seen how deadly a wire strung between two trees was earlier that day. The unlucky lady was the first to die, and the way her mouth flapped open, then shut as the wire sliced open her throat, would haunt Mark for the rest of his life.

However long that would be.

Why the fuck did I agree to this? Crowe thought as he leapt over a shrub. The tip of his boot grazed it, causing the prongs to rustle. Another gunshot sounded and the trunk of a tree next to him exploded, showering the man in splinters and damp wood.

A dull, vibrating rumbling on his left slowed him. It sounded like a roar, but it was too deep, almost indecipherable to be from an animal. A frown creased his brow as he tried to figure out what it was. He'd heard it just after it began, the game, and thought it could've been a waterfall. The only problem with that idea was that he'd been all over the jungle, as best as he could tell, and discovered nothing.

Had he finally found it?

Changing directions without a second thought, Crowe forced himself towards the thunderous sound. It reminded him of the dull roar of the subway and how a subwoofer pulsated with the beat of the bass. It helped to calm him. The sound gave him a purpose now.

All he had to do was make it to the waterfall. Once there, he could dive into the cool water and hide until the first light of dawn appeared.

Pain exploded across his vision, a blinding burst of white as a bullet tore through his right calf. The 9mm round severed his tendons and muscles before lodging deep in the bone.

Crowe screamed out in agony before crashing to the ground.

He was so close!

Ignoring the feeling of defeat that crept through his body, Crowe pulled himself through the undergrowth. His fingers curled into claws dragged his wounded body closer and closer to salvation. He didn't care if he died; he wouldn't give them the satisfaction of killing him themselves.

"I saw him go down over here!" a voice shouted excitedly. "Carruthers winged him."

The pounding of feet slowed, and above Crowe's head, he saw beams of light sweep back and forth. His tormentors were almost upon him now and any second, they'd find him.

"That wasn't me," the man called Carruthers said. "A shot like that had to come from either Charles or Perkins."

As they continued to talk, Crowe pushed himself on. Time slowed, darkness formed around the edges of his vision and the urge to stop, roll over and accept his fate became more and more attractive to him. It was over and the only thing he could do was make sure he went out with a smile.

"He's here!" the first man bellowed as his light found the still crawling Crowe. "Goodness gracious! He's still moving."

"Impossible! Nobody's made it this long and still continued to persist."

"It doesn't matter," an upper-class voice said with a sneer. It came not from behind, but from in front of Crowe. Slowing his pace, which to the wounded man felt like he had stopped, he looked up and gasped. "Hello Mark, long time no see," Charles Roy Pendleton said.

Swallowing a sob, Crowe shook his head in disbelief. They cheated.

"No, we didn't cheat," Pendleton said with a chuckle. "We're just very good at what we do. But you did well too, Mark. Don't think you failed." As he spoke, the leader of the group of men drew a large Bowie knife from its sheath.

Weakly, Crowe lifted his hand. It was a pointless gesture, but his instincts had taken over.

The large man, moustache impeccably styled, crouched in front of him, gripped the outstretched arm and plunged the blade deep into Crowe's side.

Warm blood gushed from Crowe's mouth as he gasped in pain and fright. Pendleton's eyes, dead themselves, stared at the confused face for another second before standing.

"Well, another successful hunt," he said, stepping away from the dying man. "I must admit, though, these last few have been rather tiresome. Wouldn't you agree?"

"Bordering on the banal, I'd say."

"My wife's book club has more thrills than this."

Before any of the others could speak, Pendleton rubbed his face, using a kerchief to wipe away the sweat and grime of the day's activities. "Gentlemen, we need to up our game."

Crowe's mind went blank and his last breath was a faint rattle in his chest. Nobody would mourn him or come looking for him. The only people who knew what befell him didn't care at all.

As the first rays of sunlight peeked through the trees, Pendleton nodded to himself, then said as he walked away from the body, "Let's head back to the club, yes? Drinks are on me."

CHAPTER TWO

The fire roared, sending embers up the chimney, providing plenty of warmth for the group of men. Even though it wasn't necessary, tradition and their own sense of style made them gather around it, holding one hand in front as if that alone would keep them warm.

Around them, the main room was decorated like an old Victorian hunting lodge. Old portraits of past members hung from the walls along with the taxidermied heads of animals, many long extinct.

From speakers mounted in the corners of the enormous expanse of a room, Mozart pumped through at an innocuous level. It was just loud enough for it to be heard, but not overpowering, and the men were thankful for their host's good taste in music.

"Does everyone have a drink?" Pendleton said as he entered the room. He'd changed out of his safari outfit and now wore a smoking jacket, looking very much like to the manor born.

Walking through the group, he nodded politely at them as his eyes took in their expectant faces and full glasses. It made him happy to see the usual suspects. But every once in a while, Pendleton wished for someone new to attend, to bring a fresh perspective to the proceedings and make life interesting again.

Stopping in front of the fireplace, he stared at the dancing flames and thought about the last hunts. Each were successful, as had all since his great-great-grandfather discovered the island. But the most recent ones left him feeling bored and unfulfilled.

"Lads, we have a problem," he finally said, still keeping his back to the men. "And I believe you all know what I'm referring to."

He listened to the low mumbling of the men and knew what they were thinking. It was obvious since there was only a handful, including himself and Carruthers, who took the hunts seriously. The others treated it like a day at the golf-course; get it over quick enough then enjoy food and drinks at the club.

Thinking about it sickened him.

"Really, Charles, there's nothing wrong with the hunts," a younger man, Eddington, said. "You've always made them a ripper good time. Right, fellas?"

"That's not the point," Pendleton said, forcing himself to smile at the group. "Aren't you bored with the constant wins? Don't you wish for a challenge? We need to push ourselves, or else what is the point?"

His eyes scanned the faces, studying the way the men shifted their own gazes or looked away. It was clear to Pendleton they didn't care. They were happy with the status quo and, unless he reinvigorated the hunts, he'd stop them completely.

"What do you have in mind, Charles?" Carruthers asked from his place at the back of the group. His years spent in Kenya hunting had made him a worthy game warden for Pendleton.

"It's simple," Pendleton said as he sipped from the ornate glass. He winced from the burn of the scotch before saying, "We need to make the hunts more challenging."

The other men nodded in agreement before their leader said, "But how?"

"We could give them weapons of their own? At least then they could defend themselves against *them*," Eddington said, shivering from the thought of the local wildlife. He was new to the hunts, the son of one of Pendleton's father's oldest friends.

Eddington groaned from the slap up the back his head from a rotund man in a leather vest. Finaughty shook his head and puffed on a large, thick cigar. The constant plumes of smoke gave him a cartoonish look. As he spoke, the deep rumble from his chest made everyone listen.

"You want them to fire back at us? Idiot boy. No, the best thing we can do is take the beasties out of the equation. Just keep it between us and them. No outside forces."

From the back of the room, Carruthers chuckled. "And how do you want to keep them at bay?"

"You'll figure it out," Finaughty said, looking at Pendleton. "Charles, let's not overcomplicate this. It's supposed to be a jolly good time, and if you give them weapons, we'll be the ones to suffer."

The man's point was valid, and Pendleton agreed with it. Unfortunately, there was no way to cage the animals. Apart from the loss of time and the expenses, there was the risk of bodily harm.

No, there had to be another way.

"Of course," another man said with a sly smile, "we needn't do anything so drastic except change the parameters of the hunt itself."

"Please, go on," Pendleton said with an encouraging gesture.

"You've always used the people from your offices, or people in need of money. Desperate people who have nothing to lose. That's the problem."

It made sense, and as the man spoke, an idea came to Pendleton. He could feel the smile creep across his face, pushing his moustache hair up his nostrils. For some reason, he'd always used the dregs of society and people nobody would miss. That meant they had no skills and could easily be tracked or food for the animals.

Pendleton blinked, forcing himself back to the present conversation, and he saw the men deep in discussion. Each of them had their own ideas of what to do and how to go about it, which was good and all, but they always forgot one thing.

Pendleton's island, Pendleton's rules.

"Gentlemen!" his voice boomed, silencing the men in one go. He raised his hands and spoke.

"Our esteemed friend here is correct. It doesn't matter if we give them guns, or take away the beasts. We would still cut them down in record time. The challenge, the thrill of the hunt, that's what we're missing. So, how do we get it back?"

From the back of the room, Carruthers spoke again. "Better prey."

"Exactly," Pendleton said. "We need to find men and women who have the training and skills to keep us on our toes and provide us with enough entertainment that it wouldn't matter who gets them. Us or the island."

He beamed at the men, waiting for the rousing cheer he knew was coming. But after nothing but silence, he frowned and looked at the faces.

"What if they win?"

Each man cringed and tried to escape the laugh that came from their host. The sound was without warmth and sounded like a squeezebox in need of repair.

"That will never happen," Pendleton said, wiping a tear from his cheek before continuing. "Whomever we get, we shall place a guarantee that all will lose. My word of honour on it. Good enough?"

The gathered men mumbled their approval, though they gave it begrudgingly. It didn't bother Pendleton. If they refused the idea, he would wipe the slate clean and bring in new members. *I might even do that*, he thought, but there was still one problem.

"Where are we going to find such people?"

"You can't pull them from the street or the armed forces, Charles!"

Pendleton knew they were right. It was the only problem he could see, but if he needed months to figure it out, so be it. Time was unimportant to a man like him, as long as he got what he wanted.

"Charles, I may have the solution."

The men parted as Carruthers made his way towards Pendleton. He gripped a tablet, keeping it out of sight and reach from the others.

Reaching out, Pendleton took the device and unlocked it.

Immediately his eyes widened, and he grinned at the sight of a series of dossiers. Scanning the screen, he sighed and said, "Perfect. Make it happen."

CHAPTER THREE

LAS VEGAS, NEVADA

Sean Marshall used the damp cloth to rub his face and neck. He hated Vegas, the desert, and the people who populated the city. There was something about the types who migrated to Sin City that rubbed him the wrong way. He didn't understand the need to gamble or get hookers.

It takes all sorts to make the world go round, he thought as the moisture from the cloth helped to cool him.

The muffled groans and scraping of boots made his eyes snap open. "Never a moment's peace," he mumbled before turning his head slightly.

A man and woman, bound back-to-back, their mouths gagged by rags and electrical tape, glared at him. It had been a simple job. The man had done the usual and offered to pay him more if he walked away. But the woman, she was a piece of work. She'd launched herself at him from the bedroom, shrieking like a banshee, brandishing a broken bottle and aiming for Marshall's face and neck.

"Listen, luv," Marshall said to the gagged woman. Her right eye was already swollen shut, but her left glared at him. "You can give me the stare all you want. But I've no interest in you. Professional or otherwise."

The man laughed, then winced in pain from the headbutt the woman delivered without a second thought. The coconut-like thunk made Marshall smile and chuckle.

"Here's the thing," he said, getting back on track. "The moment you came at me with that makeshift weapon of yours, that was it. See, my Pa taught me never to hit a woman. Never. But that broken bottle, well, that's a deadly weapon and I'm positive you meant to do me grievous bodily harm. That's why you're trussed up. Not my fault."

Satisfied with his own explanation, Marshall went back to the task at hand, waiting for the local police to show up. He'd done his job, subdued the target and made sure he, now they, were ready for transport. It wasn't a glamorous job, but it was better than security for some pop star, stuck-up actor or worse, a politician.

9

He'd seen too many of his ex-service mates get into the bodyguard gig and within a year, they'd already turned to the drink, or worse. At least being a bounty hunter meant he could still put his skills to use.

Glancing at his watch, he figured the cops were at least another fifteen minutes away. *Why the hell do I get the babysitting jobs?* he thought, closing his eyes again. Darkness was better than his current surroundings.

A cheap room in a cheap motel on the outskirts of Vegas. If the intelligence on the target was right, then the only reason Marvin Peck had picked this place was because nobody would've thought to look for him here. But, with all the money he allegedly embezzled from the Galindo Cartel, Marshall expected at least some hired protection.

Instead, I get a schmuck and a bottle-wielding-banshee, he thought and wished for a drink.

A buzzing interrupted his thoughts and, reaching into his pocket, Marshall swiped the screen of his phone and held it to his ear. "Is this my soul I hear?"

"You're nowhere near as funny as you think," Brody said without hesitation. His manager was the only person Marshall knew that didn't have a sense of humour. But there were moments he wished the man knew what a smile was.

"Thanks, I love you too."

"You done with Vegas yet? Can I get the payment out of escrow now?"

"Just waiting for the transportation to arrive. Need proof of capture?"

The other end of the line went quiet for a second. Even though it was standard practice to snap a picture of the target in custody, sometimes a client didn't care; confirmation would be enough. But even still, Brody was the meticulous kind of prick to make sure they didn't get screwed out of payment on a technicality.

"Brody?"

"There's nothing in the job about proof," the other man grunted. "But send it anyway. And get the Vegas PD to snap a pic as well."

Marshall nodded as his eyes focused on the back of his hand. The puckered scar tissue ran from the middle of his hand up towards his wrist, where it ended just before the sleeve began. It was a painful reminder of the past, the pitfalls of trusting another man to have his back.

"You listening to me, Sean? Oh, for fuck's sake! Are you there, you mick prick?"

His pale blue eyes blinked rapidly as Marshall forced himself back to the present. "I'm here. What were you saying?"

"Lucky you're a hard worker and deliver. You goddamn military types always come with baggage. I don't fucking know why the hell I work with any of you bastards. And don't tell me it's because of the money. I can make the same working for my brother in Jersey."

As his manager talked, Marshall held the phone away from his ear and thought about using a headset. That idea was pushed away quickly; he hated using them. Too many terrible memories. He let the angriest man he knew rant and rave. *Gotta keep the status quo*, he thought while eyeballing the bottle of Bulleit Rye Bourbon sitting on the mini-bar fridge.

"What I was saying," Brody continued without pausing for breath, "was this. You up for a couple of quickies? A few came through today."

Marshall knew better than to take on rush jobs and his desire to drink vanished. Usually there wasn't enough time to properly plan everything, which meant mistakes were made and someone died.

"You know my stance on those."

The snort sounded distorted through the phone and, for an instant, Marshall hoped Brody wasn't using again. That was the last thing he needed, but there was nothing he could do about the man's own guilty pleasures.

"I know, I know, I know," Brody said, dismissing his partner's objections. "Just hear me out, okay?"

"Have I hung up yet?"

Marshall could hear the smile in Brody's voice as he said, "Good lad! Now, these need to be done before the end of the week. All for the same customer, too. Shall I go on?"

"If you must."

"Oh, I must, I must! I don't have access to the files yet. They'll send them once you've accepted, but it looks like they want you specifically for the jobs."

Raising an eyebrow in surprise, Marshall's training kicked in. He hadn't been operating long enough to have earned a reputation. The only people who knew about him properly were recommendations from his old COs back in the UK. Even then, he was loathe to agree to the job, and Brody knew this.

"I take it from your silence that you're not interested?"

Sean Marshall sighed. "You know me too well, buddy."

"Will five hundred-thousand per body do the trick?"

CHAPTER FOUR

CARRIZO SPRINGS, TEXAS

The sun was already blistering hot, and Marshall could feel his shirt sticking to his skin. It didn't matter how high he cranked the air-conditioner, the oppressive heat overpowered the luxuries of modern man. Marshall didn't know how anyone could stand it, let alone make the journey from Mexico to the American Dream by foot.

But not having lived anywhere like Mexico or experienced it, he couldn't comment and always avoided the issue with other hunters. He had a purpose, and that had to be in the front of his mind.

According to the file, the first name on the list, known only as Alvaradejo, was the most dangerous bounty he'd ever come up against. The only problem was that nobody had a picture; just that he was a freelancer working for the Sinaloa, Sonora and Los Zetas cartels. That made the target more dangerous than others, but also gave Alvaradejo a mystic White Whale appeal to bounty hunters.

This was part of the reason Marshall had come fully prepared for a gunfight. In the back of his SUV was an M4A1 carbine, a Glock 17 handgun and enough flashbangs to put down a charging rhinoceros. He didn't want to go in guns blazing, but from all the intel he'd been given, he might have to kneecap Alvaradejo and then worry about some medical attention.

"What the fuck?"

Dark, billowing smoke rose high into the sky. That wasn't good. It was rumoured the cartels used Carrizo Springs as a dumping ground for any bodies that had to disappear from Mexico's side of the border. If that was true, then the smoke was a mass grave set on fire.

Speeding up, his right hand checked the 9mm handgun. It was loaded with a round already in the chamber. His thumb flipped the safety off. Marshall knew better than to go in without at least one gun ready.

Turning the wheel slightly, he brought the car round a bend, then slowed it to a crawl. He was right.

A fire raged in front of him. Someone had dug a deep hole and then dumped whatever needed to disappear. Marshall knew he'd have to get out and inspect the area. The only thing was that he hoped the local authorities wouldn't show up.

There was no logical reason for him being there since he never carried his bounty hunter credentials on him.

Stupid, he chastised himself. Stopping the vehicle, Marshall switched it off then clambered out of it.

Burning bacon assaulted his nostrils and instantly his eyes watered. The winds weren't favouring him, but at least he had sunglasses which helped. Turning around, he quickly grabbed the eyewear, then locked the SUV.

He would let nothing happen to his ride.

"Where are you, *amigo*?" he said to himself as he moved towards the inferno. Without a picture of the target, he'd have to go through the entire area with a fine-tooth comb. It was going to be a long day.

He kept his finger on the trigger guard. It wouldn't take much effort to apply pressure to it and fire. Luckily, his training was still there and his practice runs at the range with his friends in law enforcement kept everything smooth.

Then he heard the screaming.

It was a high-pitched wail of terror, definitely female and as he spun towards it, the gun snapping up ready to fire, Marshall's eyes widened.

Long thick hair flew about like a cape, pale skin covered in dirt, ash and blood trembled with each step and outstretched arms reached for salvation. The woman's naked body charged at him. Without thinking, Marshall lowered his gun and readied himself to embrace her.

The closer she got to him, the more he saw of her body. It was slim and muscular, but what drew his attention were the cuts, slashes and bruises that covered it. Whoever she was, she'd been abused by someone, and probably for a long time as well.

Did Alvaradejo do this? Marshall thought as his anger rose. He could suffer a lot of things, but the abuse, mutilation and humiliation of women was not one of those things. The moment he found Alvaradejo, he'd make him pay.

With a yelp of fright, the woman tripped, falling face first onto the gravel-covered ground. She cried out in pain and slowly lifted herself back up.

"Don't move," Marshall said the moment he was close enough to her. "I'm going to help you. Understand? Help."

He spoke slowly, like she was a terrified animal, which in a way she was. Her eyes were wide, filled with fright, but she nodded her understanding. Her hands grasped at him, and Marshall helped her stand.

"Do you speak English?"

"*No hablo inglés.*"

Marshall cursed his luck, then asked, "You don't speak it, but you understand me. Right?"

Another slow nod from the wide eyes. Under the dirt and blood, she'd be called beautiful in some circles and up close, Marshall fought the urge to glance at her exposed breasts. Taking off his jacket, he wrapped it around her shoulders and did up the buttons.

She looked down at the clothing, then smiled at him.

Ignoring the smile and toned legs, Marshall led her towards his car. He'd let her enjoy the air-conditioning and music while he tracked his target.

"I'm looking for someone. I think it was the same man who did this to you and that." Marshall gestured at the fire pit behind them. They got closer to the SUV and, seeing it, the woman visibly relaxed.

Standing next to the car, Marshall opened the passenger door. "Alvaradejo. Is he here?"

The woman nodded, then pointed without hesitation. Following the digit, Marshall saw a collection of shacks. If his target was there, it would be a quick and easy hunt.

"*Gracias,*" he said before helping her inside the vehicle. He turned away and began walking towards the collection of metal and wooden shacks. The 9mm pistol felt good in his hand, but there was something bugging him. A nagging feeling at the back of his head.

You'd think, he thought as he moved further away from the SUV, *that hearing the name of her attacker would get a stronger reaction.* All she had done was nod and point. Why didn't she scream, cry, or breakdown?

"Because," Marshall said as he spun, "Alvaradejo is a woman!"

He watched as his car roared to life and sped away from him. He'd been played perfectly, which he had to give due credit. It took a lot to get past him.

But there was one thing Alvaradejo hadn't taken into account.

The SUV got about thirty metres from him before his anti-theft system kicked into action. From inside the car, a loud bang sounded, blowing out the windows that was followed by a blinding flash. The flashbang he'd rigged to the ignition had gone off since she had hot-wired the car.

Walking over to the now stationary vehicle, Marshall saw the unconscious woman slumped against the steering wheel. Trails of blood oozed from her nose and ears, but her breathing seemed fine.

"That's one."

CHAPTER FIVE

LEXINGTON, KENTUCKY

Marshall felt out of place as he walked into the bar known only as 'The Bar'. He hadn't much time after delivering Alvaradejo to the local authorities to get his ass to the home of bourbon and his favourite TV show, *Justified*. While waiting with the unconscious woman, he'd received a message from Brody. All it said was: GET TO KENTUCKY, ASAP.

As the door swung shut behind him, his well-trained eyes scanned the wide-open space, clocking the other points of entry and exit. That took all of two seconds.

There was a stairwell that led up to the second floor where the backroom gambling took place. Next to it was the storage room and the toilets. On the opposite side of the jukebox, a sight he enjoyed a little more than he should've, was the emergency exit.

Taking slow, deliberate steps, but keeping his body relaxed, he counted the number of patrons and staff. One bartender stood behind the bar. Her slim frame and flowing locks made her look younger than she actually was by ten years. Out on the floor were another two waitresses; obviously the woman behind the bar was playing keep up based on how she dressed.

The only thing Marshall didn't like was the lack of a bouncer. Every other bar he'd ever been in, whether in the USA, the United Kingdom, Ireland or even Canada, had at least one large intimidating man to keep the peace.

At The Bar though, nobody.

Odd, he thought as he slid onto an empty stool at the bar. He kept his shoulders and arms slumped, ready for anything, but his legs were tense.

"What can I get for you, honey?"

Looking up from his thoughts, Marshall smiled at the lined yet pretty face. "Double of Pappy van Winkle, please." It paid to be polite. Even to a bartender.

"You're not from around here, right?" the woman said with a slight giggle. She waited for an answer before fetching the requested beverage.

"Is it that obvious?" Marshall said, feigning disappointment. "I thought I'd finally blended in with the natives."

A laugh was the only answer he got as the woman spun expertly on her heel, snatched up an empty rocks glass, then stepped up onto a small stool. Even with the added height, she had to stand on her tip-toes to reach the high-quality hooch.

"Double, right?" she reaffirmed before pouring the golden liquid. The small nod from Marshall was answer enough, and she tilted the bottle. "Where you from? Has to be pretty far with that sort of accent."

"Says the pretty lady with such an interesting accent of her own," Marshall countered, as he sniffed the bourbon. He'd never had anything like it before, just the standard bourbons everyone carried; Jack Daniels, Bulleit, Southern Comfort and Maker's Mark. But there was something almost mythological about the Pappy to him. It was a particular spirit he needed to taste before death and was so glad his second target made that a reality.

The blonde laughed again and swatted at his hand playfully. "I'm not interesting! Born and bred right here in Lexington," she said, leaning towards Marshall and giving him an ample view of her bosom. "So, where you from, sugar?"

"Northern Ireland," Marshall said as he let the ambience, music, and delightful smells wash over him. "A small town called Derry. Nothing like anything you've got over here, though."

Before the woman could continue the conversation, a grunt of pain stopped her. It was quickly followed by the sound of a body tumbling down the stairs and a second later, a bloodied body crashed into a table. The man shuddered, spat blood, then collapsed.

"You might want to get the bouncer," Marshall said, trying to be helpful. He had a pretty good idea who was causing the ruckus.

"That there sorry mess trying to figure out which way is up is the bouncer," the bartender said with a hint of anger in her voice. Her face was flushed, nostrils flared, and it looked to Marshall like she was ready to fire the poor man.

Lowering the glass, Marshall opened his mouth to ask the appropriate question when another man appeared on the landing. His hulking frame swayed back and forth. The stupid grin plastered across his face gave him the look of a wild animal, and his bloodied hands didn't help with the image.

"Dammit, Walt!" the bartender snapped. "How many times I gotta tell ya not to beat on poor Arlo! Y'know he's not right in the head, and you're not making it any easier on him."

Marshall lowered his head, not wanting to draw attention to himself, but used his peripheral vision to keep track of the man he was after.

Walter Dillahunt was dangerous, according to his file. But in Marshall's experience, there was a lot not mentioned in the file that could sway the job.

"Not my fault he doesn't know when to stay down," Dillahunt slurred as he stomped towards the bar. "Ya not going to believe this, but he said I couldn't drink and play no more. You believe that?"

The way he spoke, it had the same twang as the bartender. Another local boy, Marshall surmised. That made everything harder for Marshall. Chances were some of the other patrons might rise to help. He'd have to play it cool for now and hope luck was on his side.

"Still gives you no right to go crippling the boy!"

Each step brought Dillahunt closer to the bar and Marshall, who could smell the booze wafting off of him. Maybe he wouldn't have to fight him. In Marshall's experience, sometimes all it took was just that one extra bit of booze to send someone over the edge.

It was a crazy idea, but he had to try.

"Horseshit!" Dillahunt spat before giggling like a child. "You know that without me, my money and contacts up in Louisville and Frankfort, you'd just be another whore giving out six-dollar blowies in some trailer park. So, don't go telling me what I can and can't do!"

The movement was subtle, but Marshall's trained eyes saw the bartender reach for the weapon hidden under the bar. He hoped it wasn't a sawn-off shotgun. That would kill the drunk, voiding the contract. The only way he got paid was if he brought in the contracts alive.

Another added layer of difficulty.

"Ya not gonna fire that scatter-gun, darlin'," Dillahunt said, leaning against the bar. "It'll make too much mess and you might wing Mister Flirt here," he added, gesturing at Marshall.

Before he could respond, his target lurched forward, slipping on spilt beer. His eyes went wide and his arms spun wildly as he tried to stop his forward momentum. But his own weight and gravity dragged him towards the stool between him and Marshall.

Using his foot, the Irishman slid the seat out of the way, then in one smooth motion, stood and caught the falling man. Then, without missing a beat, Marshall spun and sat the confused drunk in his place.

"That was incredible!" the bartender cooed as she released the weapon under the bar. "You could do shows!"

Ignoring the woman, Marshall felt the old tingle along the back of his neck and dropped to his knee. Above him a chair swung wildly, and seeing the stunned look on Dillahunt morph into one of anger, Marshall grinned before rolling out of the way.

From his peripheral vision, he saw his target launch himself at the other man. At the same time, he brought his knee up and drove it into his attacker's groin before bringing his elbow down.

A dull crack sounded, and the man dropped to the ground, blood oozing from his nose.

Getting to his feet, Marshall saw five large men readying themselves for a fight. They hadn't been there before, chances were they'd been upstairs playing cards with Dillahunt. Seeing them now, he wondered if it might've been better to let his target slam his head against the bar.

"Listen, fellas," Dillahunt said, smiling meekly at the anger-filled men. "Before any of you say it, I wasn't—"

"You fucking cheat!"

"You ain't going be disrespecting 'The Bar' no more."

Marshall stepped back, making sure he wasn't going to be in the line of fire, and watched as Walter Dillahunt sighed, turned to the bartender and said, "Pour us a shot, darling." After he had his drink, he wiped his chin and winked at Marshall.

"Feel free to join in, Seamus."

CHAPTER SIX

Before anyone knew what was happening, Dillahunt took three long strides, and ducked under the closest man's reach. As he came up, he slammed the shot glass into his opponent's face. Blood shot from the wound and the man squealed like a stuck pig.

Rearing his hand back, Marshall's target drove the glass deeper into the man's face, then twisted it for good measure, ignoring the horrid, agony-riddled screams.

"Who's next?" Dillahunt's face was split by a massive grin. Lifting his arms, he readied himself for another attack. "How about you?" he said, pointing to the biggest of the bunch, who growled and tore the sleeves of his flannelette shirt off.

"I've broken wilder stallions," Dillahunt chuckled as he pushed himself off the bar and tackled the other man.

Both crashed into a table filled with empty beer steins and shot glasses. The flimsy wood groaned, then splintered under the weight and force of the two men. With a spectacular explosion of glass and wood, the table shattered.

"Oi!" one of the other men shouted, turning to Marshall. "You're with that asshole, ain't ya?"

Making his face look as innocent as possible, the Irishman shook his head. "No, sir. I just came in for a drink. That's all. I don't want trouble."

From under the behemoth, Dillahunt wheezed, "Seamus! Be a pal and get this log off of me!"

That was all the other men needed to hear, and with malicious grins, they turned towards Marshall. It didn't matter who they attacked, Marshall realised as his mind went back to his pub days in Derry and Belfast. These men were like sharks. The moment they smelt blood, it was a frenzy.

That meant the only thing Marshall could do was go on the offensive.

Gripping a chair, he hurled it at the nearest two men and, not bothering to see if his aim was true, then picked up a beer glass and threw it at another man. The glass shattered upon impact and the man screamed as his forearms were sliced open.

Dropping low, he ran towards the last man standing and his mind went to that moment in *The Princess Bride* when the hero had to fight the giant. The giant made a comment about only fighting one man instead of a group and how that changed one's tactics, and Marshall agreed with him.

His training gave him an edge, but lately nearly all of his targets were one on one. He hadn't fought a group in a long time, and even though he was good, Marshall was no Mickey O'Neil.

But taking out three of the four made it easier for him.

The last man's face was frozen in a look of stunned disbelief. Obviously, he was used to fighting in a group, not on his own. A fact that Marshall picked up on quickly and used to his advantage.

After closing the distance in seconds, he threw his arms out and wrapped them around the thug. Using his momentum, Marshall wrenched the man to the right, then left, letting go at the last moment.

The man spun, tripping over himself until his head collided with the side wall. He slumped to the floor, unconscious.

Getting to his feet, Marshall felt hands grip his arms and legs. A second later, his lower back exploded in pain, making him wince. Turning his head, he saw the man with the cut-up arms driving his fists into his body while the others held him.

"Once we've had our fun," the injured thug snarled, "you're gonna get tarred and feathered, boy."

"Leave 'im alone!" Marshall heard the bartender order. But it was useless. These guys were the town thugs, nothing more than bullies, and he knew that if he didn't do anything quick, he'd be royally fucked.

"Who the fuck are—" the man's voice became a gargled gasp before he dropped to the floor. Blood pooled from the bullet hole in his neck and his vacant eyes stared up at his still living friends, who instantly released Marshall.

Turning, Sean Marshall saw the dead body, then looked up and frowned.

Standing at the entrance were five men. They were all dressed in black tactical gear and looked like an overpowered tactical unit. But the thing that made him worry were the masks they wore. They were blank faces, similar to what Delta Force wore on a mission.

Each of them held a Heckler & Koch HK416D rifle, with a Beretta 92FS handgun strapped to their hips. They meant business, but there was no way of knowing what it was.

Who are these guys?

"Mister Sean Marshall?" a calm sounding voice asked before the armed men stepped to the side. A man dressed like a hunter smiled at Marshall, then said, "Where's Mister Dillahunt? You're not being paid to dance with the locals."

His piercing blue eyes made Marshall feel uneasy. But it gave him something to use if he had to track this guy. There was something about the way he spoke and moved that reminded him of someone, but he couldn't put his finger on it.

"Well? I'm waiting."

"Who the fuck are you?"

Slapping his head, the newcomer laughed and said, "You may call me Carruthers, and I work for the same man you do."

Brody? Marshall thought, then dismissed it quickly. His manager would never double book bounty hunters. That was bad for business and meant more money was spent. No, these guys worked for someone else.

"Mister Marshall?" Carruthers said with a small wave. "Come back to us, Sir. We need your assistance in finding Mister Dillahunt... Unless you don't want to get paid?"

As if on cue, Dillahunt's head appeared from under the large man's arm and he gasped for air. "Seamus, thanks for the fucking help! You're more useless than a one-legged man in an ass kicking contest."

He stopped talking the moment he saw the armed men, then instantly pointed at Marshall. "That's him, officers! He just went crazy and attacked these fine gentlemen. I'll cooperate fully and testify against him for you."

Carruthers chuckled, then snapped his fingers. Two of the black-clad men walked over and pulled Dillahunt out from under the unconscious man. They were silent the entire time.

"Thanks!" Dillahunt said, then turned and walked away.

He got three steps when the metallic screech of a slide being yanked back sounded and he stopped, then turned to face everyone. "I'm innocent, I swear!"

"Take him."

"What about my pay?" Marshall said as he watched the armed men grab Dillahunt and drag him back towards the door. One held the barrel of his pistol at his head, the perfect way of making anyone behave.

Not bothering to answer, Carruthers checked his phone. "Take Mister Marshall too. He'll add to the fun."

Stepping back, Marshall's mind raced, trying to figure out the best way to get out of 'The Bar' and his present situation. Unfortunately, the rifles made it harder, and he knew they'd not hesitate to shoot.

So, he did the only thing he could: raise his hands and turn around.

"Very good," Carruthers said, then dialled a number on his phone.

"How the fuck did you track me?" Marshall asked. He was genuinely curious about that since he made sure he only used burner phones or the old flip-phones that didn't have GPS capabilities.

Holding up his phone, Carruthers turned it to show Brody's nervous looking face. "Say hello to your boss."

Stepping forward, Marshall felt ready to tear his manager's throat out. He'd been betrayed, for what?

"Sorry, Sean. I needed the money. You know how Rocco gets."

Marshall knew all about Rocco Moltisanti and his loan-sharking racket. He also knew about Brody's gambling habit and how he kept amassing debt after debt, loan after loan, and that there was no way out for him except ceding control to Rocco.

That would've made sense. This, though, was worse.

"You're fucking dead," Marshall growled, then winced. Looking down, he saw a dart embedded in his chest and watched as its contents emptied into his system. Instantly, his vision blurred, and he felt dizzy.

"Damn son, that looks like a fun trip," Marshall heard Dillahunt say a second before darkness embraced him.

CHAPTER SEVEN

Marshall's head felt ten times too small than it had any right to be. Groaning, he shook it then immediately regretted the action.

It felt like he'd been on a week-long bender with the boys from his old squad and was now paying for it. A part of him missed it, but he was getting on in years and his body couldn't handle such rough treatment anymore. Not when he took into account the torment he'd inflicted upon it with training and countless missions.

"Focus, you cunt!" his old CO's voice filled Marshall's ears and the fuzziness surrounding him dissipated. His eyes screamed in protest at the jagged shards of light assaulting them. It reminded him of his SERE training, and a small smile crept across his lips.

All he needed to do was find something to focus his mind on. Anything that would give him a direction. A goal to aim for that would keep his mind clear and let him figure out a plan.

Carruthers, Marshall thought as he conjured the image of the man responsible for his predicament. But first, he needed to figure out where the fuck he was and how to escape.

That's when he heard the roaring.

He'd been too groggy to notice it before. Now he could hear the whirring of engines mixed with the rumbling and whooshing of the outside world. Marshall closed his eyes and let his ears do all the work; the engines sounded distant, on opposite ends of each other, and the rumbling was definitely wind. The gentle swaying motion, almost like a bobbing up and down, could only mean one thing.

I'm on a fucking plane.

A smile crept across his face as Marshall opened his eyes once more. The light wasn't blinding now and the more he put things together, the clearer he could think.

Turning his head slowly, Marshall's eyes took in the grey and black shades of the interior of the cargo plane's hold. He was being transported. Which meant whoever was in charge didn't want him dead.

Not yet anyway, Marshall thought as the numbness left his body. Whatever sedative they'd pumped him full of had finally worn off. Now it was time for him to break free, kick some ass, then escape.

He tried looking down, but a thick military grade strap kept his head locked in place. *Not a problem*, he thought as he flexed his fingers. They responded, so he tried lifting both arms. Again, he felt the same kind of material keeping him imprisoned.

"Fucking great," Marshall muttered as the realisation that he was immobile washed over him. Making a mental note to tear Brody a new asshole when he got out, Marshall's next action was to figure out a plan.

Turning his head from left to right, Marshall was able to take in the cargo hold properly. In front of him were other seats. The same thick straps crisscrossed the back of them and he could barely make out the backs of heads and arms of others.

At least, for now he wasn't alone.

Tilting his head as far up as he could, Marshall saw the armed guards. Each of the men wore the same black and navy-blue tactical gear and masks as the goons that attacked him before.

Actual badasses, Marshall thought as his eyes studied the closest man's weapons. He held an AK-74 automatic rifle. It was an interesting choice, but the gun held more firepower than that of the standard and more famous AK-47.

The fun I could have, he thought, trying to hide his smile. It would take some doing to get free, but if he could grab a tactical knife from one of the guards, it'd be a simpler job. As he continued planning, the lights dimmed, plunging the cargo hold into darkness.

Quickly, Marshall looked about, keeping track of the men and, happy they weren't going to shoot them, he looked at the floor. It hadn't moved. Another good sign. So then why the darkness?

A slight whirring filled the air, and ahead of the prisoners, Marshall saw a screen unfurling. It reminded him of a cinema screen and the moment it was completely opened, a projector started and the image of a man with a very large and ornate moustache appeared.

This is the guy in charge, Marshall concluded before the image spoke. It made sense, and now he had a face to focus on. Once he got a name, then this piece of shit wouldn't stand a chance.

But he looked familiar, which annoyed him.

"Welcome, ladies and gentlemen," the man said and his voice sounded tinny and odd through the plane's poor speakers. "Allow me to introduce myself. I am Charles Roy Pendleton and you have all been recruited to participate in the adventure of a lifetime! Aren't you lucky!"

A small smile crept across Marshall's face as he slid deeper into his chair. He knew who was to blame for his current situation, and nothing on the planet would stop him from making Pendleton pay. But first, he needed as much intel as he could get, which meant that for now he needed to play along.

CHAPTER EIGHT

Pendleton was waiting for someone to ask a question. At least that was how Marshall read his face. Even though the screen flickered from the bouncing and trembling of the aircraft, it was clear that a lot of cash was spent making sure their 'host' could be seen and heard.

Even with the guy's name, there was something about him that Marshall recognised. But he couldn't place his finger on it, which irritated him, but he hoped that wherever they were going, Pendleton would be there.

"Forgive my rudeness," Pendleton said with the air of royalty. "Introductions are in order."

He nodded and with a shuddering shake, the chairs turned so the prisoners faced each other. Then, with a low groan, as if on a rickety rollercoaster, Marshall felt himself pulled back until he had a good view of the others, and he cursed silently.

He recognised Dillahunt, who smiled happily back at him. Performing a quick count, Marshall saw there were another fifteen men and women locked in place, all looking equally perplexed by the situation.

Only one man seemed calm. A giant in a three-piece suit stared at a woman. Marshall recognised Alvaradejo, and she looked ready to tear as many throats out as needed so she could escape.

"Everyone, say hello to your bosom companions for the next twenty-four hours," Pendleton said, chuckling. "Some of you may recognise each other, which is bound to happen since you're all the same. Thieves, killers, and, in general, villains."

Not me, Marshall thought as he scanned the faces of the others. He recognised a few, but not enough that he needed to worry. Right now, he was more focused on getting out of his confines then finding Pendleton.

"Shall we?" Pendleton said as he stared at the screen. His eyes darted back and forth, probably reading from a teleprompter, Marshall reasoned, then smiled.

This was all rehearsed.

"First on the list is Arnold Beaumont. Nothing special about him except that he spent ten years in one of Australia's most dangerous prisons and walked away without a scratch," Pendleton said, then shook his head. "Mister Beaumont, care to share with the group, why is that?"

A small, meek looking man shook his head then bit his bottom lip.

"Probably because he knows what a knife is!" Dillahunt laughed at his own joke before looking at the others. Most joined in, except for a Japanese man covered in tattoos, the giant and Alvaradejo.

Marshall looked at Beaumont and instantly knew this was a man who worked solely on instinct. He was dangerous, in the same way a wild animal was.

"Maybe once you get to know each other then," Pendleton said with a shrug. He cleared his throat and signalled someone to do something, then waited patiently.

Using the silence to his advantage, Marshall looked at the others and quickly summed them up. Nobodies. In a fight they would flee or turn on each other, which, depending on what they were walking into, could be a good thing.

"Jessica Hoskins, say hello to everyone please," Marshall heard Pendleton say, and focused on a woman. Her platinum blonde hair was messy, yet she smiled politely at everyone and even winked at the man covered in tattoos.

"Miss Hoskins here used to be a Madame in Belgrade. She had some troubles with a gang and was found bathing in their blood. Who knew that Elizabeth Bathory still lived?

With a giggle, Hoskins said, "I'm positive I don't know what you're referring to." She winked again at the Asian who stiffened from the attention. A high-pitched witch cackle came from the woman.

"Moving along, we've got Mister Geoff Wright. He's your basic thug and jack of all trades, right, Geoff?"

A man with a face covered in pimple scars laughed before speaking. "Nothing basic about me," he said, before going silent.

Watching the group, Marshall figured they would die sooner rather than later. It was the same when he was in the service. He learnt quickly how to spot the blowhards and washouts quickly, but he felt these men and woman could be useful. He just didn't know how yet.

"Hey, hoss," Dillahunt called out to Pendleton before trying to wave at the screen. "Who's the suit over there? He looks scary."

Pendleton frowned at being interrupted, and Marshall cursed himself for getting distracted so easily. There was no way of knowing how many names he missed following a trail of thought, and he forced himself to pay attention.

"Walter Dillahunt," Pendleton said with a sly smile. "Former Delta Force operator, now a drunken bagman for the Dixie Mafia. I'm sorry, but you had a question for me?"

Interesting, Marshall thought, focusing his eyes on Dillahunt. At least now he maybe had an ally. Anyone with training like that was useful, and if his intuition was correct, he'd need all the help he could get.

"Yeah, sorry for interrupting you. But the Hulk over there. The pretty one. Who is he?"

"Ah yes," Pendleton said as he waited for the teleprompter to catch up. "That's Oleg Bekmambetov. An agent for the FSB who works for the Solntsevskaya Bratva. He's also known as the, what was it, Oleg?"

A low rumbling growl came from the suited giant. It was clear he wasn't happy with being disturbed. Looking away from Alvaradejo, Bekmambetov rumbled, "None of your business, Charles Roy Pendleton. I know who you are."

For a brief second, Marshall thought Pendleton was going to stop transmitting. His left eye twitched. "What do you think you know?" he finally asked in a low unimpressed voice.

"You are Charles Roy Pendleton. Current Chairman of the Board and owner of PenTech." As Bekmambetov spoke, Marshall noticed the others lean forward like they were trying to hear the deep accented voice better. For him though, he recognised the name of the company and everything made sense.

"Not only are you rivals with Elon Musk, but you also have contracts with the US Department of Defence, and the British Government. You rank as one of the most powerful and influential men in the world. Yet there is never any scandal about you or your family. That is you."

"An excellent report," Pendleton said, then pursed his lips. "Moving on though, the lovely lady Oleg was staring at is Senorita Frederica Alvaradejo. You'd not have heard about her, but know she is on the CIA, FBI and the DEA's most wanted lists. That should tell you all you need to know about her. Any questions?"

The group of prisoners were silent; it seemed that after the Russian's moment in the spotlight, a damper had been put on the proceedings.

"How much for her?" Bekmambetov asked, before licking his lips.

Alvaradejo ignored him. She was too focused on Marshall. Her dark eyes stared daggers at him, and it was obvious that given the chance, the hitwoman would make him suffer before killing him.

"Let's move along," Pendleton said with a weak smile. It was clear that the Russian's intentions rattled the man in charge, and he was quick to move along. "Ah, here we go. The tattooed gentleman, no, not you Oleg. The man sitting silently, looking like a statue is Joe Tanaka. One of the top men for the Shibukawa Yakuza clan in Japan. Tanaka-san is not a man you want to cross. Just ask the poor fools in the Hamna clan."

Marshall's eyes found Tanaka and he instantly knew, without a shadow of a doubt, that even though he looked like nothing amazing, this was a man more dangerous than himself and Dillahunt put together.

Hearing Pendleton humming softly, Marshall looked back at the screen. An evil grin spread across their host's face and Pendleton said, "There's one of you who is different. Not your average villain, but a man equal to all of you."

At once, the group of prisoners started looking around, trying to spot whoever was being talked about.

"Sean Marshall, formerly of her Majesty's SAS. He's now a bounty hunter working out of the west coast of the United States, and he's been responsible for some of you being in this very situation. That's what we call irony."

No, that's what we call fuck you, Marshall thought as he felt death stares fall upon him. In one fell swoop, Pendleton had guaranteed that he would be the first to die no matter what the situation was, so Marshall did the only sensible thing.

"Why are we here?"

CHAPTER NINE

"Excellent question, Master Marshall," Pendleton said. "You must be a natural leader, with a mind like that."

Marshall fought the urge to reply. If the man on the screen had intel packets on everyone, it made sense that he'd know about what happened in the services. Which didn't matter, not anymore at least, but it still ached whenever it came up and Marshall knew it was a tactic the moustached man could use to throw him off.

But it wouldn't work.

"Get on with it," Dillahunt whined. "I've got to get home for dinner and my stories."

Pendleton glared at him; his face turned red while his knuckles became white. This was a man not used to being ignored or given directions to. Which was useful to know, and Marshall squirreled it away for later.

"Very well," the man's voice was stiffer now, as if he was fighting the urge to react. Pendleton cleared his throat then said, "What's the one thing you all desire? That one thing that every single man of you wants above all else?"

It was an interesting question, and Marshall knew what he wanted. But not being like the others around him, he couldn't answer for them.

"That woman," Bekmambetov said, his focus still on Alvaradejo and Marshall made a mental note to make sure he didn't try anything.

"A shitload of money!"

"Margot Robbie!"

"A 1969 Dodge Charger!"

As the men and women continued shouting out what each of them wanted, it was clear to Marshall that Pendleton had a different answer in mind. The man on the flickering screen watched the bound men and women, a small amused smile playing on his lips making Marshall want to pummel him even more than before.

Finally, Joe Tanaka spoke. "Freedom," he said, before going silent again.

"Very good, Tanaka-san," Pendleton said with a grin. "You're completely correct. You all want freedom; whether it comes from not being chased by the law, money, or possessions. Now, what if I told you

I could give that and more and all you have to do is survive for the next twenty-four hours? Sound good?"

The stunned silence that came from the group of men and women shocked Marshall. There was a part of him that was curious to know if the man behind the screen actually had anything of value for him.

"I take it from your silence that you're curious to know more? Excellent!" Clapping his hands, the moustachioed man picked up a large tumbler and drank from it. He wiped his mouth, then said, "What I'm offering is one-hundred million dollars, tax free. A brand-new identity, should you require, and your freedom. Win the game and you walk away, never to be troubled again by myself or my associates."

Marshall heard the low murmuring of excitement before looking at the criminals chained around him. He could see they were already spending the money in their minds.

Savages, he thought before the lure of the money crept into his mind. It would make his life easier, though.

No. Shaking his head, he focused on the task at hand: finding out as much intel as he could.

"Well, that is a mighty pretty offer," Dillahunt was saying. "But me Pa always told me, if a lady offers to suck your cock for free, check for an Adam's apple. What's the catch?"

A frown creased Pendleton's brow, which made both Dillahunt and Marshall smile. The Irishman made a note that their captor didn't enjoy being spoken to in such a manner, which meant he could use it against him.

"What a colourful expression, Mister Dillahunt," Pendleton said, trying to cover his annoyance. "The catch, as you put it, is simple. You'll be dropped off shortly—"

"And don't call me shortly," Dillahunt said before cackling at his own joke.

Nobody except Marshall caught the curt nod from the man on the screen. Looking at Dillahunt, Marshall watched one of the armed guards walk over to the still laughing man, lift up what had to be a cattle-prod, and touch the end against the metal chair.

Electricity crackled as Dillahunt howled in pain while his body arched from the current. Both of his hands curled into fists as steam rose from his skin.

"That's enough." Pendleton's words were law and the sizzling sound ceased. All eyes were on the now panting and slumped man, who trembled slightly. "Any other additions, Walter?"

Dillahunt stayed quiet, the lesson learnt, but Marshall could tell he wanted to kill someone.

"Excellent! Now, as I was saying; you'll be dropped off soon and then all you have to do is survive the next twenty-four hours. If you are caught, then I'm afraid it's game over for you. The last man, or woman standing wins and will live the rest of their life like a king. Or queen."

There was something about the way he spoke that made Marshall even more suspicious. It sounded like Pendleton was purposefully avoiding the specifics of his 'game'.

"What does 'game over' mean?"

"My dear chap, game over is game over. You don't have to worry about the repercussions. Just survive and you get your life back," Pendleton said, directing his gaze at Marshall's general vicinity.

The Russian growled before saying, "Spit it out, little man. What is point? Why should we run from men like you?"

Leaning forward, Pendleton gave a wolfish grin before speaking. "You are going to be hunted. If any of my associates or myself catch you, you will be killed. Oh, and I must add, your death will be up to whoever finds you first. Me? I'll just shoot you. The others? Hard to say. Now," he stared at the group through the screen, "is that incentive enough?"

Marshall couldn't believe his ears. He was responsible for some of these people being in this situation and his own boss had set him up as well. *Sumbitch must pay*, he thought before flexing his wrists.

He felt the bonds tighten again. He was stuck until the drop off.

"Excellent. Get them ready."

The lights dimmed and Marshall felt himself tip forward. At the same time, the chairs rose until everyone's legs were dangling freely. A little down from him, he could hear Alvaradejo whimper and start praying in Mexican Spanish while Dillahunt whooped and hollered like a cowboy.

Feeling the blood rush towards the front of his body, Marshall's eyes widened at the sight of the floor splitting in half before slowly opening.

The roar of the wind filled the cargo hold, drowning out the panicked screams of the others and Pendleton's calm voice. A second later, a fine mist appeared from the edges of the door, floating in the space.

Looking up, Marshall saw a green light appear above each man or woman before they were released. They passed through the mist and disappeared from view.

His chair vibrated, and the Irishman knew that any second now, it would be his turn. He was fine with that. His training kicked in and he focused on his target and new goals.

Survive the drop.

Find Charles Roy Pendleton.

Get home safely.

His chair shuddered and closing his eyes, the last thing Sean Marshall heard was Pendleton's farewell, "Good luck!"

CHAPTER TEN

Marshall knew High Altitude Low Opening (HALO) and High Altitude High Opening (HAHO) jumps from his old life with the service. He enjoyed them, the rush of adrenaline as he and the others in the squad timed everything perfectly, the thrill of knowing that if anything went wrong, it meant an ugly death.

But those were always controlled. They were given oxygen tanks, altimeters and radios to keep in contact. What Marshall was doing right now, free-falling at similar speeds to that of the HALO jump, without a mask, any controls, or a way to gauge his distance from splattering the ground, was insane.

Which was the reason why he was enjoying it so much.

The air bit and whipped around his hands and face. Any piece of exposed flesh was victim to the cold. But as he shot through the clouds, Marshall felt more alive than ever before.

His vision was blurry from the wind and he felt dizzy from the ceaseless spinning, which was an easy fix. Extending his arms and his legs out, he steadied himself and quickly surveyed the situation. All of his HALO training came back to him with the most important being: breathe.

Looking left, then right, Marshall saw the others. Like him, they were still strapped to their chairs, but now he noticed the small packs that bulged from their fronts and looking down, he saw the same on him.

That had to be the parachute!

His eyes darted about and he watched, as best as he could, the others wildly spinning, their faces scrunched up in panic. He could barely hear their frantic cries for help and saw some struggling to free their hands.

As far as Marshall was concerned, that was a mistake. There was no way to know if they were heading towards another trap, jagged rocks or a dense jungle. Trees were as much a threat as any manmade weapon. For now, he'd risk turning into human stew over getting impaled.

Forcing his chair onto its back, he could just make out the plane's trails. The thin tendrils of cloud that the wings disrupted gave the sky an eerie beauty, and for the briefest of moments, Marshall wished he had a camera to take a photo.

Get your head back in the game, he chastised himself before looking about. He needed to see how many were tumbling out of control. Though that was an easy count; all of them. Which made sense since it was impossible to gain control of a falling brick. He chuckled at the image that appeared in his mind before frowning.

His ears focused on a high-pitched banshee-like wail and craning his neck, he saw one of the chairs plummeting towards him.

"Fuck!" Marshall mumbled as he rocked back and forth, hoping his weight would shift the chair. If it didn't and the other crashed into him, it would instantly kill both people.

Slowly the chair wobbled, then tilted as the approaching prisoner's screams became clearer. It was a woman's, but to him, the sound she made was similar to that of a monster. Squinting again, Marshall saw it was Alvaradejo.

The woman's hair stood up, whipped about by the rushing air, and Marshall saw her face properly for the first time. No wonder the Russian was attracted to her, but for the Irishman, she wasn't the be all or end all of beauties.

Just another deadly woman.

Looking down at his bound hands, Marshall leaned forward and gagged. The strap around his neck was still there, but it wasn't as tight as before. That was good, and feeling relief wash over him, he started flexing all of his muscles. If he could loosen at least one of the straps enough, then he could slip free and work on the others.

The only thing that was a problem, and it was a big problem at that, was the fact he didn't know how far up they were or how close to the ground he was. Without that knowledge, Marshall needed to work fast.

Ignoring the shouts and begging for help from the others, he continued working on his freedom. The moment he looked up at another plummeting man or woman, he'd forget what he was doing and try to save them. It was his biggest weakness and had caused him problems in the past.

"You have to save everyone in your squad," his old CO told him time and time again. Which made sense back when he was in the service. But now?

It would get him killed, for sure.

As he worked at freeing himself, a low droning started up. It reminded him of a helicopter, but that was impossible and looking, he saw nothing but the falling people.

The sound continued to grow louder and louder.

Closing his eyes, Marshall focused on the sound, then gasped. It wasn't a single sound but multiple versions at different frequencies. And as he continued listening to it, he heard a hiss that could only come from an animal.

Birds don't hiss, he thought as he opened his eyes in time to see the petrified face of another man.

"It's a mons—"

The man's words were cut off as something large and leathery flashed past him. The speed was unbelievable and Marshall couldn't make it out, but when it vanished from his view, it was clear that whatever it was, it was dangerous.

Where the man's chest once was, now all that remained was a gaping bloody wound.

Looking about as best as he could, Marshall saw the others scream in terror as the air was filled with the droning of wings flapping and the hisses and growls of large predators.

They were under attack and unable to do anything about it!

Whatever they were, they sliced through the air like torpedos, and for a moment, Marshall thought he saw a long protruding beak and a hard crest rising up from the head. But that was impossible and only a—

He flinched and screamed as the chair released him and the pack attached to his body opened, flinging him up, then back like a pendulum.

Shaking his head, Marshall grabbed the parachute's controls, then spun in the air. His eyes darted about and he sighed at the sight of the other parachutes opening one by one. At least now they had a chance of surviving.

Then he heard a bird-like screech and turned to his right.

CHAPTER ELEVEN

Lifting his legs, Marshall readied himself to kick out at whatever creature was speeding towards him. He could barely see it through the clouds, but the screeching and growling made it clear it wasn't a bird.

Marshall counted the seconds until he could lash out, but at the last second, the monster darted down and he saw large translucent wings flapping.

Then a wail of terror that became gurgling as another man died.

Looking about, Marshall saw more of the large creatures ducking and weaving through the clouds. They moved too fast for him to see. Part of him knew what they were, but the logical part of his brain didn't want to believe it.

He couldn't believe it.

Focus on landing, he thought. Having a goal helped him keep focused. Without it, his growing fear would win and he'd be at the mercy of the attacking monsters.

A man yelped in fright, his boots barely missing Marshall's face. Reacting instinctively, he reached up, grabbed one then pulled hard, sending the man spiralling off course.

He bellowed in terror as Marshall watched the parachute's lines tangle. The wail of panic continued, fading, as the man vanished from sight.

Marshall saw the poor soul shoot through a large cloud bank, breaking up the moisture and droplets of water. Below, he could see the tops of large trees.

They were above a jungle!

A second later, one of the monsters darted past him, following the tumbling man into the clouds and Marshall saw it properly and he laughed uncontrollably.

It was a pterodactyl!

"Of course, it would be," Marshall said to himself as he forced his mind to accept the fact that they were being attacked by dinosaurs.

A victorious scream filled his ears. Looking about, Marshall saw one of the creatures approaching. Blood covered its beak and flesh dangled from the claws. The dino had fed and was now ready for seconds.

A grin appeared on Marshall's face and he lashed out with his feet.

The pterodactyl grunted in pain as his foot connected with its beak and the animal wobbled in the air before dropping.

Feeling proud of himself, Marshall looked down and took in as much of the terrain as he could. This was imperative if he was going to survive, and he remembered his early days of training. Without knowing the lay of the land, his chances of survival were limited.

There was no way in hell he'd die here. He would make sure of that.

A high-pitched scream filled the air, and he saw Alvaradejo careening through the sky. She was still locked in her chair, and two of the flying dinosaurs were trying to grab her.

Lucky girl, Marshall thought the moment he realised that the only thing saving her were her restraints. But if she wasn't freed soon, then her death would be messy.

With a grunt, he used the parachute's controls to move himself towards her. A quick glance down told him he didn't have a lot of time, but he had to try.

Of course, he reasoned as he moved closer to her, *that was only if there were more dinosaurs waiting below*.

One of the attacking dinosaurs rolled, blood spurting from a gash on its chest and with a shriek of pain, it flew away. A second later, the other pterodactyl bellowed in rage, then pushed off and away from the tumbling chair.

Its left wing struggled to move, and it took Marshall a second to spot the piece of metal sticking out of it and he whistled, impressed.

Moving his eyes back to the woman, he saw bright blood staining her clothes. Her eyes were bright and without hesitating, she pushed herself away from the chair and easily opened her parachute.

It had been a ploy.

Clever girl, he thought as he watched her vanish behind the clouds. He felt like an idiot. Once again, she'd played him. That couldn't happen a third time, especially if she used it to get the advantage.

But there were more important things for him to focus on.

Like the flying dinosaurs attacking everyone else.

Looking about, Marshall did a quick count and realised that four of them were dead. The rest were injured to certain degrees. Blood trailed from the unconscious bodies and he knew the dinos would finish them before they hit the ground. That meant there was only one thing he could do.

A low rumbling came from behind him and, spinning, Marshall felt sharp claws scrape his chest. He winced and lashed out again.

His foot hit nothing but air and he screamed in anger.

A second later, the dinosaur spun in the air and made a beeline for him, its beak glinting in the early morning sun. It looked majestic and dangerous at the same time. Each time it flapped the massive wings, it picked up speed, signalling it was aiming to kill the dangling man.

"Not today," Marshall mumbled as he waited. Timing was everything and if he was off by a second, then he'd be food or a bloody stain.

At the last moment, the pterodactyl rolled so its clawed feet could grab him. That was what he was waiting for and seeing it, Marshall pulled on the controls while spinning his body.

The dino passed him. A frustrated growl came from it and the beast flapped its wings, pushing itself forward and away from Marshall, who yelled in victory and flipped the animal off. That was twice now he'd avoided death.

A shadow passed over him and a second later Marshall heard a ripping. The world spun, becoming a blur as he lost control, flipping like a kite in a hurricane.

Looking up, Marshall's eyes widened at the sight of a series of tears in the parachute's canopy. He was fucked, if he was lucky and looking down, he saw trees race up to embrace him.

Before he crashed into the jungle, a single thought came to him, and it made him laugh and think, *Of course, the dinosaurs wouldn't get me, but a fucking tree would.*

CHAPTER TWELVE

"They've already landed. Or at least should be landing in the next few minutes," Charles Roy Pendleton said, waiting for the men to take their places in the viewing room.

As the men funnelled in, they each sat on a plush leather seat and placed their drink down on a table next to the chair. On top was a crystal ashtray and the men who smoked lit up without a worry. Like the rest of Pendleton's compound, luxury was the defining principle.

Pendleton waited until the last man entered, then closed the doors and slowly made his way to the front of the room.

"Gentlemen," he said the moment he reached the front of the room and stood below the blank screen. Once he was finished and the others were ready, he'd signal the boffins to start streaming.

"Gentlemen," Pendleton said again, making sure he was heard. "Gentlemen!" he snapped, and this time, the group of men ceased their talking and stared at him. "Thank you for your undivided attention," this got a laugh, and he smiled.

Finaughty shook his head then rumbled, "Get on with it, Charles. The sooner I lay my money down, the sooner I can enjoy myself!"

A few of the others mumbled their agreement, but all knew that the rules and traditions couldn't be rushed or ignored.

"Of course," Pendleton said with a low, supercilious bow. He disliked the rotund man, but he always bet large and was as much a fixture of the hunt as the Pendletons or even the dinosaurs.

"As I was saying. We all know why we're here. The hunt! But the question I pose for each of you individually is this: what brought you here? What was it that made you decide to pay for membership and inclusion in such a group that not even Zuckerberg, Musk, or Bezos could gain entrance?" Before any of the men could answer, Pendleton held up his hands and said, "There's no need to answer. Just keep that in the front of your minds, gentlemen."

Continuing his spiel, Pendleton made sure his gaze fell upon each seated man. He wanted them to be aware that they were there by his grace alone, and that even a braggart like Finaughty wasn't as important or as powerful as he thought.

"What you're about to witness, yes, is a hunt. But unlike the ones that came before, our prey is talented. To paraphrase a movie, they all have special skills. Let's see how special they actually are. Shall we?"

Going silent, he allowed the men to have a moment to ponder what he said and for their excitement at the coming blood to grow.

Charles Roy Pendleton was a natural showman.

"We've spared no expense in bringing them here, and you have my word that the show will be unlike anything witnessed in over sixty-five million years."

Eddington giggled like a child, then sank into his chair from Pendleton's glare. He knew the young man was going to be a problem, but not like this. Then again, he reasoned, everyone reacted that way when it came to their first time.

"As per usual," Pendleton continued, "we shall let the native wildlife thin the numbers to something more manageable. Once that's done, which, considering the quality of prey, should be within the first twelve hours."

Another man cleared his throat, the sound echoing throughout the room, disrupting Pendleton's speech. He couldn't be sure if it was on purpose or accidental. But the constant interruptions made it clear to him he needed to speed up.

"In saying that," this was the moment he enjoyed more than anything else, except his first and last kills, "shall we make this interesting?"

At once, the men cheered and leapt to their feet. It didn't matter how long he talked for or what he said, the moment money was brought into play, their attitude changed. Only Carruthers refused to bet on the outcome of the hunt. But that was his prerogative.

Finaughty was the first to place his wager. "Five million that the Jap survives until the thirteenth hour."

"Seven says he makes it to the last four!"

"You're writing checks your account can't handle, Hawthorne!"

The men laughed as they placed their bets and made private wagers. It was all in good sport, adding an extra level of excitement to the proceedings. Naturally, at the end of the hunt, all debts were collected and then Pendleton would get his cut.

The house always won.

"The Russian," Eddington said, struggling to be heard. "I bet he goes after that Mexican within the first hour."

Hearing his wager, Pendleton raised an eyebrow as he calculated the odds of that happening and her reaction to it. "How much?"

Not expecting the question, the young man blinked as his mouth hung open. Seeing his opening, Pendleton made sure the others heard his wager, "Ten million that he makes an attempt within the third hour.

Another ten, if he succeeds and another ten, that's thirty million total, if she fights him off. Do we have a wager?"

He watched the young man's eyes dart about, looking for a saviour or out. The others knew better than to bet against Pendleton. Especially when it came to those amounts, but Eddington was new and needed to be taught a lesson.

"Thirty million," he said, puffing up his chest. "Done... I'll also wager that the bounty hunter makes it to the final hour."

The confidence in the young man's voice made the others stop talking and turn to watch the bravura performance.

Pendleton's smile grew larger. He was enjoying himself immensely and stepped off the raised platform. Even though he was now standing on the same level as the others, he still towered over Eddington.

"Again, how much, young Eddington?"

The young man swallowed nervously, then said a little too quickly, "Whatever you think is fair."

"Your life," Pendleton said without missing a beat. His eyes were focused on the confused man, but he could feel the disapproving looks from the others. He crossed a line and if he didn't play it properly, he'd lose them.

Nothing ventured, nothing gained, he thought, while waiting for a response.

"What?"

"You heard me. Your life is the wager. If you win, you're safe. I win? You enter the next hunt. Do we have a deal?"

"Charles," Finaughty snapped as he pushed his way between the two men. "You go too far! No man in his right mind would ever make such a wager, and you should keep in mind that without our connections and influence, this would've been taken years ago."

Slowly, Pendleton turned his gaze from the young man to the large man. "You're absolutely right," he said after a tense minute. "Where are my manners? All wagers must be for dollar amounts and valid for the duration of the hunt. Anything outside of that," he looked pointedly at both men, "is between the parties and their gods."

Turning away, he bounded up on to the platform, then faced the men once again. He knew he needed to smooth things out and make sure they understood nothing was wrong with him or the hunt.

A task easier said than done.

"Lads," he said and waved for the group to sit. "Feel free to change amounts and whatever other details you see fit over the course of the hunt. Until then, eat, drink and be merry. And as they say, *game on!*"

CHAPTER THIRTEEN

Sean Marshall's head snapped up. The back of it crashed into the trunk of a tree. He groaned in pain, then looked around. It was a move he wished he hadn't made.

His parachute, or what was left of it, clung to the branches. The snag swung him out and his return trip resulted in the head injury. But that wasn't his only problem. Quickly he judged he had to be at least twenty metres up, with nothing but more branches to help break his fall.

See, he thought, *this is what happens when you try to help others.*

It was a valid point, but at the moment, it did nothing to help. His primary objective was to get safely down and start moving. A part of him suspected that Pendleton would show up at some point. That meant he could take cover and wait for the man to make his entrance.

Easier said than done.

The first order of business was to get free of the chute and find a safe way down. The operative word being safe.

Looking down at the pack on his chest, he saw that the pterodactyl's claws had slashed it open. Blood oozed from the wounds and he winced after taking a deep breath. Once down, he added to his list of things to do, the first order of business would be to check the wound properly. He couldn't risk getting an infection in the middle of a jungle.

Gently poking and prodding the pack, he saw the straps were made from the same material that held him in place on the plane.

Reaching behind his torso, Marshall followed the straps until he found where they met. Gently, his fingertips traced the shape, poking and prodding the mechanism that locked them together. Closing his eyes, he let his mind conjure a picture in his mind.

It wasn't useful.

Sighing in frustration, he looked around at his surroundings. Yep, it was a jungle, but the types of trees, thick vines and the humidity made him think they were somewhere tropical. Close to the equator.

Great, he thought before glancing down again.

As he yanked on the straps again, he looked up at the sky. Through the jungle's canopy he couldn't see much except for small patches of sky. That was good. The dinosaurs wouldn't be able to attack, the branches made it impossible for their beaks to get through.

Dinosaurs, the word and image of the flying monsters came to his mind, and Marshall laughed.

Not even twenty-four hours ago, he was chasing bounties and living his life. If you could call it a life. Now he was being hunted and chased by dinosaurs. Reality and logic were gone, and he found himself in a horrendous situation that nobody would ever believe.

At least until you get them drunk enough, he thought, as the sounds of the jungle gave way to a deep infrasonic rumbling that shook him to his very core.

"What the fuck was that?" a familiar voice said, and Marshall looked down.

He couldn't see anything, but slowly he made out the sounds of feet stepping on branches and dead leaves. It had to be the others, and from the lack of echo, they were close.

"Doesn't matter," the Russian's voice drowned out the rumbling easily. "What does is winning. Out of Oleg's way."

Listening to the sounds of people struggling, Marshall's eyes scanned the area. If he could find anyone friendly, then there was a slim hope they'd help him.

He felt the vibrations before the fabric ripped. Marshall's head snapped up and his eyes widened. He hadn't thought about the possibility of the parachute breaking!

Making lemonade from the lemons life gave him, the bounty hunter reached up and, gathering the ropes, he yanked on them. His eyes focused on the growing holes and tears in the fabric. At the same time, he pushed his feet against the tree. It was a position that would give him greater leverage and allow him the ability to fall on his own—

The branches above and below him snapped, and he fell.

CHAPTER FOURTEEN

The moment he crashed into the ground, Marshall rolled, coming up onto the balls of his feet. He crouched into a wrestling stance, ready to take on anyone who attacked him. If it was Pendleton, one of his goons, or one of the other prisoners, he'd make sure they'd die screaming.

Unless it was another dinosaur, in which case his only option was to run.

Turning in a small circle, he slowly lowered his hands as he saw the others staring at one another. Each of them wore the same expression; confusion mixed with disorientation.

"Hey, Seamus! What the fuck did you get me into?"

Dillahunt stalked towards Marshall. His hands curled into tight fists and the man's eyes screamed for revenge. "I have one lousy drink with ya and look at me! I almost died!"

Before he could get close enough, Marshall dropped and swiped with his leg. His shin connected with the back of Dillahunt's legs, and the larger man tumbled to the ground.

A quick punch to the diaphragm and Dillahunt was incapacitated.

Staying quiet, Marshall looked at the others. Most stared at him, all with the same distrustful and hate-filled look Dillahunt had given him. But there was no sign of Alvaradejo.

Focusing his eyes on Tanaka, the tattoo-covered man glared back at him. Even though his slight frame gave him the appearance of being weak, Marshall was positive the smaller man could easily kill him.

Better keep an eye on him, Marshall thought before holding both hands up in a friendly gesture.

Tanaka's eyes darted to his hands then back to Marshall's face. After a second, he nodded. He wouldn't attack. Not yet anyway.

"You! You are responsible for this!" Bekmambetov declared.

Before Marshall could react, two of the largest hands he'd ever seen wrapped around his arms, pinning them to his sides. The ground vanished under his feet as he was lifted.

With a roar of victory, the Russian hurled Marshall across the jungle. He slammed into a thick tree trunk before sliding down, gasping for air.

"Stand back! This is Oleg's kill!"

Just fucking great, Marshall thought as he watched the bear dressed in human clothes stalk towards him.

Quickly, Marshall rolled out of the way a second before a massive booted foot stomped where his head had been.

The giant grunted in frustration, then turned around.

"Nobody escapes Oleg Bekmambetov," the Russian said. His voice was deeper than thunder. Tearing his jacket off, his arms bulged and everyone saw the tattoos snaking up and under the rolled-up sleeves.

Scrambling backwards, Marshall struggled to get to his feet. His eyes darted about, searching for anything he could use as a weapon. Anything to even the playing field.

Bekmambetov reached out, ignoring the kicks Marshall delivered and gripped his leg. The smile he gave the bounty hunter sent a chill through everyone's spines. Oleg Bekmambetov was no ordinary killer.

"You brought Oleg here. Now you die here!"

"That's not exactly true. That was all Pendleton. I've never seen you before and honestly, I could've gone the rest of my life having not seen your hideous mug."

They were stupid last words, and Marshall didn't know where they came from. It was too late now. He'd die as an idiot.

Marshall winced in pain as the Russian's hand continued squeezing. He could feel his bones bending. Pretty soon they'd buckle, crack, then snap. He didn't want to think about a compound fracture or what was happening to the muscles and tendons inside his leg.

"Once you are dead," Bekmambetov snarled as he began dragging the struggling man towards him, "your skin will be perfect for my new coat."

Before he could say anything else, a parachute covered his face. The Russian gasped, startled by his sudden loss of vision. He released Marshall who, once again, scooted away as Bekmambetov fought to clear his face.

The giant stumbled about, unable to see or do anything except grunt and growl in frustration. But the more he struggled, the more tangled he became.

The scene looked comical, and Marshall fought the urge to laugh, like the others. Straining, he wished he could see who was responsible for the cartoonish sight.

Riding his back, pulling tightly on the parachute was Alvaradejo! The woman had snuck up on the giant and was now playing rodeo with him. Her face was set in a frown of concentration as she fought to keep upright and control of the Russian.

Marshall watched, amazed at how the woman had not only survived but also gotten the advantage. *No wonder she's used by the cartels*, he thought.

His eyes locked with hers and she nodded before launching herself forward off of the man's back. She spun mid-air, twisting the ropes tightly as she travelled downwards. Her body weight plus the disorientation Bekmambetov felt did the trick, and as she landed, Alvaradejo let go and ducked out of the way.

The Russian couldn't stop himself and as he slammed into the ground, the others erupted in riotous laughter.

"Thank you so much," Marshall said as he got to his feet. He held out his hand, ready to show his appreciation.

The woman stopped, looking at the outstretched hand before her gaze met his. Her dark eyes glistened and slowly she smiled at him. Reaching out, the woman grasped his hand tightly and Marshall smiled back at the woman.

He grunted and slumped to his knees as both hands gripped his stomach. His gut ached from the blow, and he struggled to breathe.

Seeing the woman start a roundhouse kick, he dropped to the ground in the nick of time. Alvaradejo's foot sailed through the air, passing through the space his head occupied seconds before.

Not missing a beat, her fists flew, delivering rapid hits that stung more than anything else.

Marshall's arms came up to block her hits, but each time he did, her other hand snaked out and landed a blow. He winced and grunted from the blows, and as her attack continued, he felt his body grow tired.

"You're gonna die here, boy!" Dillahunt chanted, watching the Mexican press her attacks harder. "Better enjoy the last touch of a woman. And what a woman!"

Alvaradejo's arm shot out again, but this time Marshall grabbed it. His fist closed around her forearm and she blinked in surprise. Pulling it away, he held it tight and waited.

With a snarl, the woman's other fist flew towards him, and once again he caught it mid-air.

Before she could lash out with her leg, Marshall's forehead connected with cartilage. Pain shot through his face, but it would only be momentary. He was more focused on the crack and cry of pain from the woman.

Letting go of her, Marshall shook his head, clearing his sight, then backed away. Blood flowed from a gash in Alvaradejo's forehead and she pressed both hands against it.

That's one, he thought, then turned to face the others.

The group looked less sure than before and he said, "We need to work together!"

"Get 'im!" Dillahunt ordered, pointing at Marshall. A blur of movement came from his left and the Irishman looked, then blinked in confusion.

"What the?" Marshall barely got out before Tanaka's foot cracked him up the side of his head. Bright white flashed across Marshall's vision and he spun from the hit, his world tilting at a horrid angle.

Falling, Marshall felt a fist connect with his chest and he screamed out a second before the world went dark.

CHAPTER FIFTEEN

Marshall woke with a groan. Not only did his head throb with pain, but his entire body made it clear he'd lost the fight spectacularly. The light burnt his eyes, and blinking, he lifted his hand to rub them.

The cool, damp feeling of a leaf caressed his cheek. Frowning, he pulled his hand back, then cocked his head to the side, perplexed at the sight of both hands bound by what looked like a mixture of vine and the ropes from one of the parachutes.

"Figures," he mumbled before lowering them to his lap. His eyes focused on his legs. They too, were bound, with rope wrapped around his thighs, above his knees and down around his ankles.

Tanaka or Alvaradejo really didn't want him escaping anytime soon.

There was only one thing to do: get his wrists and torso free and then worry about his legs. To do that, Marshall leaned forward and grunted. Something was holding him against the trunk of a large tree, and before he even saw it, he knew it was more of the rope.

Yep, sure enough, glancing down at his chest, he saw the twisted mixture of rope and vine looped around his torso. It was tight enough so he could still breathe, but not loose enough that he could escape easily.

"About time you woke up," Arnold Beaumont said, making Marshall look up and forget his current predicament.

Standing in front of him was Beaumont, who smiled pleasantly. He held a makeshift club that looked to Marshall like a large bone that was carved to resemble a bludgeon. It was clear the others tasked the man with making sure he stayed put.

"That's right," Beaumont said as he crouched. "The others thought it best that you had a babysitter."

"And you drew the short straw?"

"Not a chance!" Beaumont said before cackling. He pounded the ground with the club and Marshall watched it crack and slithers of bone fly. "I wanted this. You think I'm crazy enough to trust those criminals?"

Slowly, Marshall shook his head. Keeping his eyes focused on the club, his mind raced, trying to figure out the best way to get him to perform the action again. If he could get a shard of bone big enough, it would be easy to cut his way through his bonds.

"Only until they turn on you."

Beaumont nodded. A sly smile crept across his face, and a shiver ran up Marshall's spine. "Don't you go thinking that I'll partner up with you, mate. There's no way in hell I'd team up with a bastard who hauls people in for cash."

"Depends on who it is you're bringing," Marshall said, then winked conspiratorially. He kept his wrists low to his body and slowly flexed them. He needed to do it slowly. If he moved too fast, his guard would see it.

Another cackling laugh came from Beaumont, and again he pounded the ground with his bone club. Large cracks formed at the point of impact, and Marshall was positive another blow would do the trick.

Now it was only a matter of getting him to repeat the action.

"But still, you've got to admire Walter's thinking," Marshall said softly. His ears focused on an approaching sound. It was a whisper of movement, and he thought it could be Tanaka, or Alvaradejo.

"How so?"

"Well, both he and I have training enough to get through this little slice of hell. With both of us working in tandem, you'd be the ones left behind. But, by taking me out, he gets all the glory and builds trust with the others." A small smile crept across Marshall's face as he added, "Except for you, naturally."

Beaumont's eyes became slithers, and he crept towards the tied-up man. He kept the makeshift club in front of him, but his other hand was planted on the ground, to stabilise him.

It would take little effort to knock him over, but Marshall knew that if he did, the risk of losing the weapon was too great.

"What you talking about?"

Marshall sighed, rolling his eyes. He hoped his bullshitting would work, but obviously Beaumont wasn't as deranged as he thought. That meant he needed to work harder to convince him that he was on the level.

Opening his mouth, a slight movement out the corner of his eye stopped him talking.

He saw it, a few of the lower, younger ferns shaking from something moving past them and he swallowed, forcing his fear down deep inside of him. This wasn't the time to let fear control him. He could do that later.

"Isn't it obvious?" he asked, resting the back of his head against the tree. "You're not my guard, but bait."

The other man shook his head, clearly in denial, and he turned away from Marshall. "No. I volunteered to make sure you wouldn't get away," Beaumont mumbled.

"Yes, but if I'm supposed to be bait for Pendleton or whatever else is out there, then a guard isn't really necessary, right?" Marshall was playing a dangerous game. On the one hand, there was nothing to stop the other man from caving in his head, then bashing his brains out instead of doing the logical thing, joining forces.

Opening his mouth to answer, Beaumont froze at the sound of chittering. It sounded like squirrels playing and came from the right. Both men turned at the same time to stare at the brush. The leaves and branches danced and jiggled.

There was definitely something there, and it was excited.

"Don't move," Marshall hissed as the sound became clearer. He felt his heart pump faster and his breath became shallow. His training kicked in and his eyes darted about, searching for any other signs of movement.

"What the fuck is out there?" Beaumont asked as he stood and slowly walked towards the trembling bush.

The sound was louder and devoid of anything resembling a squirrel. Instead, it was a mixture of a bird's chirp and the clicking of a dolphin. To Marshall, it sounded alien but also familiar.

The more he listened to it, the more Marshall felt the desire to flee.

"Get back," he hissed at the other man. Beaumont was less than a metre away from the bush and Marshall winced, waiting for the inevitable to happen.

He heard the chirping become a snarl, then the sound of a branch snapping and Beaumont's startled yelp. Closing his eyes, Marshall waited to hear the tearing of flesh and cries of agony that would signal the man's demise.

Instead, Beaumont cackled, forcing Marshall's eyes to snap open.

"What the fuck?"

CHAPTER SIXTEEN

"What the fuck?" Marshall echoed Beaumont's question. He couldn't believe his eyes, yet he knew that what he saw was real, no matter how unbelievable it was.

The green-skinned dinosaur stood and stared at Beaumont. Its slender neck bobbed up and down like a chicken and the pitch-black eyes focused on the man before it. As it breathed, the tiny reptile wheezed, then squeaked, giving it a cute yet pathetic attitude.

Watching it, Marshall blinked. He recognised it and the name came to him. "That's a Compsognathus!"

"A compy?" Beaumont asked. He shook his head, then chuckled. "What next?" he asked before turning back to the small dino.

"Get away from it," Marshall said as he heard more chittering coming from the jungle. That wasn't the only dinosaur in the area and there was no way of knowing how dangerous it really was.

"It's kind of cute," he heard Beaumont say. "Think I could pat it?"

Marshall opened his mouth to speak but could do nothing except struggle against his bonds and watch the other man extend his hand out towards the now curious dinosaur. The small head bobbed up and down and it chirruped before moving closer to the extended pink fleshy digits.

Even though he couldn't see the man's face, Marshall was positive Beaumont was grinning like a child. But he knew that there was only one outcome; Beaumont's messy death.

"Get the fuck away from that thing."

The other man waved the club at Marshall before crouching lower so he could see the compy better.

Marshall shook his head and struggled harder. He could feel the ropes loosening around his wrists. It wasn't enough, though. As he kept going, Marshall was positive there were more of the chicken-sized dinos waiting in the wings.

Beaumont giggled as the dinosaur's snout inched closer and closer to his fingers.

The creature's eyes focused on the man and it gently sniffed at the pink flesh, breathing in and out as it got the man's scent. "This is amazing!" Beaumont said, turning to glance at Marshall.

Screaming in fright, Beaumont's legs pushed him away from the dinosaur. Drops of blood splattered the jungle's floor, staining the dirt and dead leaves as he retreated.

"It fucking bit me!"

"Of course it did," Marshall said, still fighting to free himself. Leaning to the side, he saw the dinosaur shake its head violently. In its tiny jaws was a chunk of bloodied skin, and it snarled as it lifted its head before devouring it.

That's not good, Marshall thought as the beast hopped towards the cowering man. Beaumont's right sleeve was red and Marshall wondered if there was an enzyme in the dinosaur's saliva that was affecting him.

It didn't matter though. The tiny monster stopped, then lowered its head and snarled, baring razor-sharp teeth. The sound was unnatural and both men froze, a primal instinct taking over.

Then, the compy lifted its head, making the same chirping sound as before. It looked cute, except for the blood and shredded flesh wriggling from its mouth. Studying the two men, it tilted its head back and forth.

"Cut me loose," Marshall said as the animal looked behind itself.

Beaumont shook his head. Paralysed by fear and shock, Marshall saw the paleness of his skin. Whatever was in the dino's spit, it wasn't good for humans, and that meant he couldn't afford to get bitten at any cost.

The compy made a strange sound, almost like a whistle, and Marshall looked up. Slowly, more of the tiny dinosaurs exited the jungle, first five, then another ten. More and more until he counted around thirty, identical looking except for a browning on the back or some scars from fighting.

"Shit."

Hearing the sound, the lead compy turned back to the two men. Its tiny eyes flicked between the wounded Beaumont, who shook his head weakly, then to Marshall. Was it deciding which one to feast upon first?

Who cares? Marshall thought as he flexed his wrists, forcing them apart as far as he could. The rope gave slightly, and he chuckled in victory. A small snarl silenced him.

The lead compy hopped over to Beaumont and sniffed the man's leg. Its thin tail swished the air, and it pecked at the limb. Beaumont whimpered and seeing that he wasn't going to fight back, the animal turned to its brothers and chirped.

That was the signal.

Marshall watched the dinosaurs swarm the man like locusts, covering Beaumont easily. He flinched, then groaned as they attacked him.

Blood oozed from the mound of dinosaurs, and Marshall struggled to see what they were doing. Muscle, blood and tiny teeth and claws flashed from between the constantly moving mass of dinos. The ground and foliage near were splattered dark red and Marshall shuddered, listening to the happy growls and slurping of flesh being devoured.

Then, as fast as it started, the compies were done and hopped off the corpse. All that remained of Beaumont were tattered shreds of clothing and his bones. In less than thirty seconds, they stripped him bare.

Just like piranhas.

"No fucking way," Marshall said, then clamped his mouth shut. His voice alerted the dinosaurs, and as one, they turned to face him. Thirty bloodied triangle snouts bobbed as one.

He was next on the menu.

"Fuck that," Sean Marshall said as he slipped a hand free. With a victorious grunt, he pushed the rope around his torso up over his head, then undid the ones around his knees and ankles.

He was finally free.

Scooping up a handful of dirt and twigs, he threw it at the tiny monsters, then ran for his life.

CHAPTER SEVENTEEN

Pushing past a branch, Marshall winced as it whipped his face and he felt warm blood drip from the scratch. Quickly, he pressed his hand against it, stemming the flow of blood and hoped the compies wouldn't smell it.

He didn't know where the hell he was going. All he wanted to do was get away from the hungry predators chasing him.

It surprised him how quickly they caught up to him. Then again, he was in their territory and they could navigate the jungle far better than him. He did have an advantage over them, one that Marshall could put to good use.

Crashing through the jungle, Marshall's mind went back to his training and assignments in the Amazon and Mexico. It was hard dealing with the humidity, his heavy pack and the dense foliage. But its purpose was clear, to prepare him for the hardships of being in the SAS, and he loved every minute of it.

This was different though, and he didn't know how much longer he could push himself this hard.

Luckily, the snarls and angry growls of the dinosaurs were the greatest of motivators.

He heard the scream and reacted instantly. Turning to his left, he saw the compy launch itself off a tree.

Jaws open wide, its claws extended, the dino was ready to latch onto him.

Instead of stopping or speeding up, Marshall kept the same pace and waited until the last instant. His arm snaked out, grabbing the startled dinosaur mid-air. Its slender body was slick with a film of mucus that made him gag.

The compy slipped, sliding down and before it could bite his hand, Marshall squeezed its neck before whipping it about as hard as he could.

The tiny neck snapped, and the body went limp. It was the same technique as taking out a snake, and it surprised Marshall how well it worked on the dinosaur.

Unfortunately, he didn't have time to focus on it.

Tossing the dead body over his shoulder, Marshall kept running. Behind him, the growls turned into bellows of rage.

Good, Marshall thought as he bounded over a fallen tree. Ahead, he saw a line of the tiny menaces and shook his head. If they thought they could stop him or even herd him towards a kill-box, he'd make sure to disappoint them.

Marshall leapt over them. He felt the tiny mouths nip and snap at his boots, and as he landed, he ducked and rolled under a low-hanging branch.

Hearing the pounding of tiny feet gaining on him, eventually he'd have to do something about them. That was the only problem with animals that hunted in swarms, it took a lot to dissuade them.

Ahead of him, Marshall saw a broken branch. Both ends were jagged and sharp-looking. Against the swarming dinos it was the perfect weapon. Speeding up, he made sure his feet didn't hit any roots or downed branches. At the same time, he kept his eyes on his target.

All he had to do was grab the branch as he passed it and then he'd be set. But the closer he got to it, the compies closed the gap.

Doesn't matter, Marshall thought, pushing himself harder and faster. Darkness crept into the edges of his vision and he shook his head. He forgot to breathe. If he hadn't noticed the blurring of his sight, he'd have passed out!

Gasping for air, Marshall immediately felt better, and grinned. Opening his left hand, he spun his new weapon, using the branch's momentum to get a comfortable grip.

He skidded to a halt, turning to face the coming swarm of teeth and claws. Now armed, he could take out as many as needed.

Seeing him stop, the compies sped up. Their tiny heads lowered as their jaws opened and their claws spread, ready to shred flesh.

Sweeping the branch along the ground, Marshall flung the first wave to the side. Not hesitating, he let the branch swing the other way, knocking the next group in the opposite direction and he revelled in the squeaks and dull thuds of the bodies hitting the ground.

As the tiny dinos launched another attack, Marshall stabbed at the air. His arms shuddered from the impact and he felt blood dribble onto his hands before flicking the limp compy corpse off it then stabbing the next one.

With each tiny shriek of agony, the other compies hissed in anger, their rage growing. They bounded towards Marshall, pushing themselves off the ground or from trees at an alarming speed.

He couldn't hold out much longer.

"I'm not going to die like this," he grunted as he stomped his foot down on top of a compy. He felt a sense of satisfaction as the tiny body exploded from the pressure. "I'm going to die in the arms of a buxom wench!"

As if on cue, a deep bellowing roar and the pounding of heavy feet shook the jungle. It sounded like a mixture of a lion's roar and an elephant's trumpeting, and whatever was making it was pissed.

Hearing the sound and seeing the foliage trembling, Marshall backed away. At the same time, the compies stopped their attacking and cowered, lowering their heads as they chittered nervously at one another.

Marshall smiled as he watched the dinos back away from him. It was the perfect opening to escape. But there was no guarantee that they wouldn't attack him again.

The roaring ended, its absence almost deafening, and the tiny dinos stopped their cowering before looking at Marshall again. One chirped at him and the others started to bob their heads, in the same way as before.

"Fuck you!"

CHAPTER EIGHTEEN

Crashing through large leaves, Marshall's makeshift spear caught on a vine, yanking him backwards.

Growling, he pulled hard on the weapon. The length of thick plant life held tight and with each passing second, Marshall knew he was wasting time. That was bad.

Shaking his head in disgust, it was always a terrible thing to abandon a weapon, Marshall left the branch hanging limply. With a sharp turn, he continued pushing himself through the jungle.

There was no way he'd let the tiny bastards get him.

Marshall's legs screamed in protest and he knew something drastic needed to be done or else they'd spasm, then fail and he'd collapse. Without any way of defending himself, he'd be an easy target and the compies would devour him.

"Don't think like that," he said, happy to hear a voice even if it was his own. He needed to distract himself from his situation and talking out loud, dangerous as it was, was the best option.

It didn't help his current predicament though, which was what he needed to focus on. Everything else was secondary.

His foot caught on a root, the gnarled thing tripping him, and Marshall fell.

Gasping in pain he slammed into the ground. It took him a second to recover and, pushing himself off the ground, he heard the compies sing in joy.

They saw him fall.

"Fuck this," Marshall said, as his eyes caught sight of a large tree. It looked tall enough that the dinos couldn't get to him and he was positive they couldn't climb.

But he could.

Scrambling to his feet, Marshall heard the compies behind him speed up. He shook his head. It was a stupid mistake that cost him valuable seconds.

Running again, he made a beeline for the tree and the moment he was close enough, he jumped, clinging to the lowest hanging branch.

The piece of wood groaned and, for a second, Marshall feared it would snap. Below him he could hear the compies, their tiny feet breaking dried leaves and snapping twigs. Glancing down, he saw them gather and chitter at him.

Listening to them, Marshall was positive they were egging him on. It sounded like a chant. "Fall," it said, and he laughed before hauling himself up.

The chant from below became annoyed snarls, and when he swung a leg up and over the branch, the dinos hissed.

Breathing heavily, Marshall watched the dangerous animals jump, trying to reach their prize. Each time they tumbled back to the ground, his smile grew bigger. The sight of their tiny bodies crashing to the ground, landing on top of another compy, was funny and as he clambered up to the higher branches he laughed.

Sean Marshall did it. He bested a swarm of dinosaurs, the story would be unbelievable, and with the right crowd he wouldn't have to pay for drinks.

Settling in, he used his thighs to hug a thick branch while he rested against the tree trunk. Marshall stared out at the jungle stretching before him. He couldn't see much, but it didn't matter. He wanted to get a better idea of his location and the density of the jungle.

One was easier to do than the other.

Below him he heard a shriek of pain and saw one of the compies trying desperately to climb the tree. Its tiny front paws were bloodied and he could see that the claws were broken and bent at ugly angles.

"Serves you right, ya fucking cunt," Marshall said, then waved his hand at the beasts. He didn't have to worry about them at the moment. With that problem solved, even for a moment, he could focus on the next thing.

Forming a plan to survive and escape.

He reasoned they were on an island. There was no way they'd be anywhere else. No government would allow such a place and such an activity to happen, no matter how powerful or wealthy Pendleton was. It made more sense that this was an island and from the plant life, heat and what he saw when falling from the plane, it was tropical in nature.

That meant they were somewhere near the equator. At least he hoped that was the case.

Pendleton. The name came to Marshall's mind, unbeckoned, and he frowned. That was his primary target. If he found the man responsible for his situation, he'd be able to get some much needed and healthy revenge. Of course, he continued reasoning, chances were that Pendleton had a way off the island, and that would be his next objective after getting to the lunatic.

A series of frustrated chirps and hisses caught his attention and looking down, Marshall saw the compies slowly slink back into the jungle.

"Good riddance," he said, massaging his legs. It felt good to rest and plan, but he knew it couldn't last forever.

You'll need a team, he thought, putting his mind to what lay ahead. *At least four, anything less and the danger increases exponentially. Tanaka is perfect.* He continued thinking, putting together a team out of the group of other criminals.

It was clear that Joe Tanaka would be useful. He moved silently and could handle himself in a fight. The next name to appear in his head was Frederica Alvaradejo. Her own unique skillset could be turned to getting off the island. But they needed one more.

"Dillahunt," Marshall sighed.

He wasn't positive about using them. After all, they did leave him to die by dinosaur or human. He had every right to continue on his own. But it wasn't the smartest move, and he knew it.

As he continued thinking, a low, almost silent rumbling started. He felt it in his gut and instinctively gripped the tree tighter. If he fell from this height and hit any branches on the way down, it'd be ugly.

Slowly, the rumbling became a growl that soon morphed into a roar. Marshall had never heard anything like it before and he felt terror.

Then he heard the chattering of the smaller dinosaurs, the compies, and it was clear they too were afraid of the sound. Until he needed to though, he wouldn't leave the safety of his perch.

A loud crack filled the air, and he flinched, the sound reminding him of bones snapping, then he heard the crash of a tree falling.

"Now what?"

CHAPTER NINETEEN

It took him a second to stand, but the moment he did, Marshall looked out into the jungle again.

He couldn't see much, but part of him could tell where the roaring came from. There was a chance that the others were there, and he felt a pang of trepidation. There was no way of knowing what they encountered, but Marshall was positive it was bigger and angrier than the compies.

Which meant that it was stupid to go and help them.

Shifting his weight from foot to foot, Marshall used both hands to grip an overhead branch. He felt the entire tree sway from the mixture of a gentle breeze and his own weight. It felt good, like he was back on the water and he allowed himself a smile.

A woman's scream punctured the moment of serenity and Marshall cocked his head to the side, listening intently to the sound.

Marshall frowned, continuing to listen to the screams and the roaring. He didn't know who was screaming, but a part of him was positive it wasn't Alvaradejo.

Tracking the sounds, Marshall pinpointed the general area they were coming from and closed his eyes. He needed to figure out how many of the others there were, as well as the number of potential enemies. Even if they were dinosaurs.

He knew there was at least one dinosaur. Pendleton's men wouldn't make that sort of sound. *Not unless they used speakers and voice modulators*, Marshall thought while he listened.

The dino was bigger than the compies and the way it stomped about, the thudding of feet, he could tell it was a quadruped. Which meant it was a herbivore. Finally, some good news.

Straining to decipher anything beyond the shrieks and roaring, all he could hear were more cries of fright and panic.

You need them, he thought before punching the bark-covered trunk. He winced from the blow, then looked at his knuckles. Blood oozed from the scratches and gouges that covered them.

He took a handkerchief from his pocket and wrapped it around his bloodied hand. It would do for now, and at the first chance to find some water, he'd clean it.

You need them, the thought reappeared, and he grunted.

"What if there's something worse?" he asked the jungle. It was a valid question, and he already knew the answer. There was always a bigger fish.

Sighing, Marshall clambered down. As he moved, being careful not to stab his hands on any sharp chunks of bark or broken branches, he looked down at the ground.

Still no sign of the compies.

The moment Marshall's feet touched the ground, he dropped into a protective stance and waited, silently counting to thirty again. With each number, he panned his head left then right, scanning the trees and bushes for any sign of the compies.

Nothing. Marshall straightened, then started walking towards the screaming. He moved slowly, making sure he wouldn't get ambushed by the tiny dinos.

"*Оставайся со мной, милая, я защищу тебя!*" a voice bellowed in Russian.

Stopping, Marshall tilted his head, waiting to hear anything else. All he could hear was the crunching of trees and the screaming of people.

Taking another step, another familiar voice shouted, "*Vuelve a la mierda, idiota!*"

It was Alvaradejo!

Now he had a reason to hurry, and with a shake of his head, Marshall pushed his way through the forest and towards the others trapped on the island with him.

CHAPTER TWENTY

Using his forearms, Marshall kept his head protected from the branches. It worked, but he knew his arms would be bruised and covered in cuts and scratches.

Peering through the gap between them, he was given a narrow field of view of what was in front of him. Which was enough. Every four steps or so, he turned left, then right, giving himself a wider view of the immediate area.

Whatever is attacking them, no matter how many are wounded, you only need three of them, he thought. If there were others, so be it. He'd find uses for them.

Even the Russian.

The only problem he could see was the fact that he and the others had no way of protecting themselves. Short of using branches and constantly running, which would work for the smaller creatures. But if they came up against larger predators, and he shuddered at the thought of a tyrannosaurus rex chasing them, or even Pendleton's men, they'd be fucked. And he wasn't ready for that.

Not yet, anyway.

Ducking under a branch, something caught his eye. Slowing his pace, Marshall turned to his right and saw what appeared to be a person resting against a tree. He frowned and lowered his arms, giving him a better view.

It was a person! But the way the head was slumped against his chest and the limp arms dangling on either side of the body didn't give him much hope they'd be helpful.

Could have something useful!

The thought galvanised Marshall, who jogged over to the body, keeping the direction of the horrific sounds to his back. It'd be easier for him to get back on track.

Getting closer, the familiar stench of death greeted him before he saw that the man was dead. The blackened skin hung loosely off his skull, and Marshall could see jagged scratches and punctures on his face.

A dinosaur killed him.

"Poor fucker," Marshall mumbled, then smiled. His eyes stared at the man's tactical vest. It looked pristine and was fully loaded. He'd been ambushed and counting the magazines, Marshall realised they were for a rifle, hopefully something with proper stopping power.

Crouching in front of the body, Marshall started checking the vest's pockets. They held the usual stuff; a can of pepper spray that was almost empty, flashlight, pencil and notebook, a first-aid kit which was out of date, and plenty of fresh ammunition. Without thinking, he undid the protective covering and slipped it over his head.

He had more use for it than the corpse.

This wasn't some poor cunt, Marshall thought as he searched the man's body and pockets. With gear like this, he reasoned, the man was one of the hunters. He must've been attacked, then left out in the cold by the others, and that meant there could be other discarded bodies and equipment out there.

"Excellent," Marshall said, as he found a large knife and a canteen. Holding it to his ear, he shook the container and chuckled at the sound of water sloshing about. It was still full. He popped the lid and sniffed the opening.

A foul smell greeted him, and the momentary feeling of relief vanished. It used to be water, but now, the liquid was tainted and undrinkable.

"Fuck," he muttered as he tossed the metal container away. It didn't matter. He knew there had to be a water source, a river or stream that he'd be able to drink from and clean his wounds.

Right now, though, he needed to get moving. He could hear more voices shouting over the roaring, which now sounded like a rhythmic rumbling, and the clearest one was speaking in Spanish.

Listening to the voice, Marshall continued patting down the corpse, then stopped and laughed.

Under the corpse's right arm, he found it. A strap and clasp connected the weapon to the body, but the gun was familiar to him. Undoing the clasp, he gently pulled the H&K MP5 submachine gun out and inspected it.

Just by looking at it, Marshall could tell the weapon could still fire, but he needed to be positive of that. Pressing the magazine release, he caught the almost full container and tapped it against the tree trunk. The dull thunk and clinking of metal against metal made him smile. The bullets would fire now.

Next, he gripped the slide and pulled it towards him as his eyes studied the ejector port. He winced from the screech of grinding metal, but it moved easily and he caught the bullet that was spat out.

Releasing the slide, he watched it snap back into place. The action was smooth, but not as much as he'd like it to be. Yanking back on it another three times, Marshall nodded when the slide moved as if it was brand new.

So far, so good, he thought as he lifted the weapon and took up a crouched firing stance. He tucked the stock into the crook of his arm and gripped it. Even though the rifle was empty, his training kicked in and he squeezed the trigger.

A loud click sounded and Marshall grinned, squeezed it another four times and, satisfied with the result, quickly slipped the ejected bullet back into the magazine before slamming it into the magazine insert of the MP5.

Attaching the strap to the vest, he made sure he wasn't forgetting anything. Patting down the corpse, he felt something leathery attached to the back of the body's pants. Unclipping it, he smiled at the sight of a SIG-Sauer P239 pistol. It really was Christmas, and unburdening the dead man of the weapon and spare mags, Marshall smiled.

Standing, the body seemed less without its gear, and Marshall felt a pang of guilt for raiding it.

"You're not going to need it," he mumbled before stretching and cracking his neck.

Turning back towards the direction of the symphony of destruction and screams, he hefted the weapon, checked that it was set to semi-auto and that the safety was on.

He couldn't risk a stupid accident.

"Now I have a machine gun. Ho ho ho," Sean Marshall said to himself before taking off at a jog. He felt more like his old self, now that he was armed.

CHAPTER TWENTY-ONE

Clambering over a downed tree, the branches and still green leaves providing ample cover, Marshall blinked and fought the urge to gasp. That was the perfect way to give away his position and even though the sight before him was awe-inspiring, he wasn't that stupid.

Armour plates covered the dinosaur's wide back with a row of defensive looking horns protruding from below where the top of the body curved. The dinosaur's belly and legs were bare, unprotected, but the speed of the animal, for something bigger than an elephant, made up for it. The mouth opened, and it bellowed before swinging the thick club-like tail through the air.

Following the direction of the attack, Marshall saw Jessica Hoskins scream before diving out of the way.

The ground exploded from the impact and a horrible image crashed into Marshall's mind, and he shuddered. At the same time, the dinosaur spun, and he saw its face. Now he gasped, since the dinosaur wasn't a carnivore.

It was an Ankylosaurus!

A tank dinosaur, as far as he knew it was a herbivore and only attacked when it was in danger or if its young were being threatened. Scanning the area, he couldn't see any smaller ones. It was on its own.

So, what made it attack?

As soon as the question formed, it vanished the moment the Ankylosaurus roared. Being up this close, Marshall covered his ears, protecting them from the deafening sound that reminded him of a truck's horn and a buffalo call. Underneath it, though, he detected a growl which set his teeth on edge.

Something was wrong here, and he needed to round up the others and get away from the rage-filled dinosaur.

Moving along the trunk, Marshall brought the MP5 up and peered through the scope. Moving the gun back and forth, he scanned the area for signs of the others. As he did, he saw a red, pulpy mess splattered against a boulder. Whoever it was, Marshall was positive they hadn't suffered much.

"*Сука*, come for Oleg Bekmambetov! I will show you what real man is!" the Russian's voice stopped the Ankylosaurus' rampage, and it snorted before turning to face the man.

Tracking the voice, Marshall found him standing out in the open, arms spread apart in a display of macho bravado. His face was calm, but his eyes and smile glistened with expectations. *He can't be that crazy*, Marshall thought, then saw movement behind him.

Flicking the safety off, he changed the setting to single-fire and squeezed the trigger.

Bekmambetov flinched, turning to follow the bullet's path. He growled in annoyance, ready to attack, but the sound became a whimper at the sight of another dinosaur charging towards him. The small triangular head shook as the spines along its back trembled and pulsated.

"Move ya ass, boy!" Dillahunt bellowed, shocking the giant into action.

Marshall lowered the rifle and watched, mouth open, as a Stegosaurus crashed onto the scene. It was beautiful until the spiked tail swung faster than he expected. At the same time, it spun, keeping its target in view.

The Russian dove to the ground and rolled as the spikes pounded the earth in rapid succession, tracking his movements.

Screaming, Bekmambetov shoved another man, one Marshall didn't recognise, into the Stegosaurus' path. He didn't have time to react and his scream was cut short as a long, curved spike punctured his chest.

Blood exploded from his mouth and he whimpered as the dinosaur flung him about.

"Stay low!" Marshall heard Dillahunt's voice and scanned the area, trying to find him. As he did, the dinosaurs continued their assault, each of them not bothering to acknowledge the other, it was as if they only cared about the men and women.

The Ankylosaurus bellowed again as its tail slammed into a tree. The tall ancient plant trembled from the impact and another man fell from it.

His scream ended as he landed hard on the dinosaur's back. Groaning, he rolled and as he tumbled, the animal shifted its weight, catching the man mid-air. He gasped and reached up, feeling one of the horns sticking through his stomach.

Before he could cry out, the animal slammed its body against the tree, smearing the man across the bark.

A high-pitched snarl caught Marshall's attention and turning to his right, he laughed.

Joe Tanaka, a makeshift spear in his hand, was attacking the Stegosaurus. He danced about, moving faster than the lumbering animal could, and whenever he stopped, he plunged the weapon at it.

Along its flank were bloodied wounds. Gouges and scratches from where he'd hit his mark, but it wasn't enough to deter the massive dinosaur. Instead, the Stegosaurus was attacking more frequently, turning so it could impale the tattooed man on one of its tail spikes.

Watching the Yakuza stab, then leap away before attacking again, was almost balletic, and Marshall wanted to continue, but he couldn't. He needed to find Dillahunt and Alvaradejo.

Lifting the rifle again, he peered through the scope and searched the area. The hulking forms of the dinosaurs made it hard to see anything through the limited view of the scope, but Marshall expected it.

That's why he kept one eye open.

"Seamus! Is that fucking you, son?"

Out of the corner of his eye, Marshall saw waving, and turning, he spotted Dillahunt cowering under a fallen tree. It was balancing against another tree and provided much-needed cover for the man and a couple of others.

Making eye contact, both men knew what they needed to do and with a nod, Marshall switched the MP5 to semi-auto. He couldn't afford to waste ammo with full-auto. Then, taking a deep breath, he rose from his position and squeezed the trigger.

CHAPTER TWENTY-TWO

The 9mm bullets sped through the air, piercing the Stegosaurus' side. Blood squirted from the wounds and the dinosaur screamed then spun in fright.

Dropping so his aim was steadier, Marshall shifted his weapon, targeting a more vulnerable spot on the dino and fired again. The bullets shredded one of the fins that regulated the Stegosaurus' body temperature, and he grinned.

He missed the feeling of a powerful gun in his hands. He had access to them as a bounty hunter, but the times when he actually needed one were few and far between. This was a treat, and he felt back in the service, on a mission, taking names and kicking ass.

The dinosaur spun, trying in vain to find whatever was hurting it, but all it did was give Marshall a wider spread of targets.

Lowering his aim, he squeezed the trigger in short bursts. He didn't want to kill the dinosaur, just wound it enough that it would think twice about following them. Each time he fired, he felt a sense of satisfaction when the dino's flesh shuddered, blood erupting from the wounds and it bellowed in pain.

It's just an animal, Marshall reminded himself. He felt guilty for enjoying its suffering. Blinking, he saw the damage he'd done to the Stegosaurus then lowered the rifle and whistled. It was loud enough that Tanaka heard him, and seeing him, the Yakuza nodded before ducking out of the way, heading towards him.

Unfortunately, the signal also drew the attention of the Stegosaurus. It turned to face him and growled.

Acting on instinct, Marshall lifted the rifle, aimed, and fired.

He saw the bullet slam into the dino and it shrieked in agony before turning and fleeing. Its girth and strength cleared the way for it perfectly and a part of Marshall hoped it would survive. After all, it was an animal long thought extinct.

A frustrated snarl came from his left and, turning, Marshall saw the Ankylosaurus. The dino was using its tail to shatter the trunk shielding Dillahunt and the others. They huddled together and flinched each time the club-end of the tail crashed into the tree.

Checking the point of impact, it looked as if the tree wouldn't last

68

more sustained blows. But there was always the chance that the Ankylosaurus would grow tired before then and do something drastic.

Lifting the rifle, Marshall squeezed the trigger.

The bullets pinged, ricocheting off the armour plating. He swore, of course that happened. He aimed too high.

As he adjusted, he heard a wail. It was high-pitched and sounded human, though he didn't know anyone who would make that sound willingly and lowering the rifle, he saw Frederica Alvaradejo and Tanaka running full-tilt towards the dinosaur.

Blood covered the woman's face, whether it was hers or someone else's, was impossible to tell.

Hearing the scream, the Ankylosaurus stopped its attack and turned to face the two charging humans. It roared, pawed at the earth, then lowered its head, accepting the challenge.

They'll be killed! Marshall thought as he peered through the scope and adjusted the focus. He wasn't the best long-range shot, but in this situation, he didn't need to thread the needle.

Breathing out, he squeezed the trigger and waited.

Alvaradejo and Tanaka were five metres away from the dinosaur, and as it roared, ready to trample them, it flinched. Blood flowed from above its right eye and it whimpered in pain.

Taking the opportunity, Marshall fired, emptying the rest of the magazine. The thick leathery skin that was a neck trembled from the impacts and after a second, blood oozed from the bullet holes.

At the same time, the Mexican and Yakuza rolled, coming up under the dinosaur's stomach. Each held a sharpened stick and, as one, they stabbed at the soft belly. They weren't strong enough to pierce the flesh, but with the wound over its eye and the stings, the Ankylosaurus bucked, then trudged away.

"Move ya asses!" Marshall shouted, making sure they saw him clearly.

Dillahunt nodded before pushing the others in his direction. The Southerner seemed at ease with directing people, and he stayed until the others were already close to Marshall. He nodded his thanks, then signalled for Alvaradejo and Tanaka to follow.

Moving his view from the Ankylosaurus trying to clear its vision of blood, and the people, he saw the confused look on Frederica Alvaradejo's face.

It was clear she didn't expect to see him again, and Marshall laughed. He had to admit that put in the same situation, he'd wear the same expression and he wondered if she'd thank him. It didn't matter.

Especially since there was the possibility most, if not all, would be dead before the end of the day.

One by one, the others clambered up next to him. They panted, energy already spent, and looked ready to collapse, but they nodded their thanks to him.

It felt good and as he smiled, Marshall heard a low threatening growl. Turning, he saw the Ankylosaurus glaring at him. Its muscles tensed and as it charged towards them, he shouted, "Run!"

CHAPTER TWENTY-THREE

The Ankylosaurus crashed into the fallen tree, and the trunk exploded. Splinters, chunks of bark, branches and leaves rained down as the group ran, trying their best to keep out of the animal's way.

Marshall was in the lead. He didn't know how that happened since he was the last to slide off the tree. But he wasn't going to argue with anyone about the position and looking to his left, then right, he performed a quick body count.

Apart from himself, Dillahunt, Alvaradejo, and Tanaka, there were another five. He couldn't see the Russian, and part of him was relieved.

Quickly, he turned back and glanced at the Ankylosaurus. The dinosaur's size and the horns sticking out of its side made it easy for it to move through the jungle.

"That's unfair!" Dillahunt said. He kept pace with Marshall easily, but it was clear from his laboured breathing that he needed a rest. Like everyone else.

Fair's got nothing to do with it, Marshall thought as he spun, his feet still moving, and fired.

Spotting the movement, the dinosaur lowered its head, and the bullets bounced off a protective armour plate on its head. Not missing a step, it raised its head, roared, and sped up. Its large nostrils flared with each breath. The sight reminded Marshall of a charging bull.

"Any other ideas, bright boy?"

Marshall shook his head. "Get away from that thing. After that, it's all academic."

An enormous grin appeared on Dillahunt's face, and he nodded. It was clear he was enjoying himself and even though Marshall didn't want to agree with a criminal, he had to admit there was something fun about being around real-life dinosaurs.

Except for dying, he thought before feeling the ground shake. Looking up, he saw the trees sway wildly, and he knew the dinosaur was almost upon them.

"Hard right!"

Hearing the command, the group changed direction as one. For Marshall, it reminded him of a flock of birds and the image of the compies came to him. The way those little bastards moved reminded him more of a swarm of locusts and he shuddered at the image of Beaumont's decimated carcass.

"We whole?"

Dillahunt nodded, then after a second shrugged. "How the fuck should I know? Want me to take roll call?"

Before he could respond, Marshall heard a high-pitched scream. "Keep going," he said before turning around. The scream was a woman's. As he waited, he saw Alvaradejo pass him. Her face was a blank mask, and he could see a gash on her forehead that needed medical attention.

"Where the fuck you want us to go?"

Marshall couldn't answer. There was no way of knowing what was ahead of them, only what was behind them, and everyone knew what that was.

Watching intently, Marshall saw Hoskins scrambling to her feet. Her mouth wide open, she screamed as she tried to catch up with the others.

Lifting the gun, Marshall was tempted to call out to her, but didn't when he saw the Ankylosaurus appear behind her.

Turning, the woman shrieked and raised her hands as the dinosaur spun, bringing its tail down. The crack of bones shattering followed by a wet squelch filled the air, making Marshall flinch.

Slowly, the Ankylosaurus lifted its tail. Hoskins' mangled body, liquified limbs flapping in the wind, dangled from the club. The dinosaur shook it and a groan came from the woman.

She was still alive!

Hearing the sound, the dinosaur roared before pounding the ground, and the woman with its tail.

Marshall saw the first hit, heard a pop similar to that of a balloon exploding before turning to flee. He didn't need to see the pulpy mess that was Jessica Hoskins. Working for the SAS, he'd seen plenty of corpses and that was one more he didn't need.

Not paying proper attention, he tripped over a gnarled root and grunted.

A growl silenced Marshall and, turning, he saw the Ankylosaurus glaring at him. The nostrils flared, and it sniffed the air before lowering its head and snarling.

"Fuck," Marshall said, scrambling to his feet. Running as fast as he could, he used the direction of the others as a guide. His ears picked up the sound of the dinosaur closing the distance behind him. Marshall hoped that soon there'd be a break in the jungle and a way to stop the still charging dinosaur.

Pumping his arms and legs as hard as he could, Marshall didn't see the cameras mounted in the trees, or the drone passing overhead.

The recording devices focused on the fleeing man, and after a few seconds of trailing him, the drone sped away.

CHAPTER TWENTY-FOUR

"No! Not the redhead! I wanted her at the end," Perkins pouted as the image of Hoskins' mangled remains flickered on the screen. After a second, the shot changed to a series of angles showing the still charging Ankylosaurus.

"You wouldn't know what to do given a chance," Finaughty said, laughing boisterously as he puffed happily on a large cigar. Since the hunt began and the live feed appeared on the screen, he hadn't moved an inch.

Perkins fell silent as the others laughed. There was always one or two that were the butt of jokes and it varied depending on who spoke first. For the rest of the men, it was all in good fun.

Next to Finaughty, Eddington looked uncomfortable with the carnage on display and he focused his gaze on the view from the drone. "How many are there?"

"We have a fleet at our disposal," Charles Roy Pendleton said, his voice startling the younger man, who yelped in fright. Ignoring the display of weakness, the moustached man sat.

"Most governments would kill for our tech," he continued proudly. "Camera resolution rivals that of any 8k camera. Battery power isn't a worry since they have solar panels installed and a program activates when the batteries reach a certain percentage."

"Crikey, that's impressive."

Pendleton nodded, satisfied by the man's awe. "As for actual numbers, that's a trade secret, old dear," he said, before clapping a hand on the man's shoulder. Squeezing it, he smiled when Eddington winced, then said, "How are you enjoying yourselves? Anything we can get for you?"

With a click of his fingers, a couple of ladies dressed in suits appeared. The other hunters wolf-whistled and admired their figures.

"Another!" Finaughty bellowed and gestured with his cigar at the empty glass. "And don't skim on the good stuff this time."

Pendleton smiled and nodded, silently agreeing with the smoking man. His eyes darted to Eddington, and he asked, "How about you, Master Eddington? What delicacies do you desire? Or is there something more physical you crave?"

As the young man turned bright red, Pendleton roared with laughter, then nodded at the women. They bowed before vanishing through an alcove. Continuing to laugh, he stood and raised his hands, silencing the other men.

"Lads! So far, I'd say it's been quite a show." He chuckled at the loud cheer to come from the inebriated group. This was what he wanted. The drunker they got, the more outrageous they'd bet, and none would notice a worrying fact.

They weren't partaking in the actual event.

"For those of you who have lost any wagers, my deepest and sincerest apologies, but you know the rules. Before you leave the island, and return to your dreary lives, all wagers will be settled. Any outstanding debts, and well suffice to say, you'll be given front row seats to the next hunt."

Finaughty groaned as he heaved himself to his feet. Wobbling slightly, it took him a moment to steady himself, and he burped loudly before speaking. "It looks like they're heading for the fields," he said, gesturing at the direction the drone was flying. "If we don't hurry and get out there, we'll miss the action, and I for one don't want to get the raps' sloppy seconds."

"Yes! I want to skin that Russian bear and mount him in my trophy room!"

"That Mexican will make a fine addition to my harem," another hunter bellowed before slipping and falling face first onto the luxurious carpet.

With a sigh, Pendleton held up his hands and waved his fingers. It took longer than he liked, but eventually, the group went silent. Only Finaughty, muttering to himself, and the snores of the passed-out man continued.

"You're absolutely right," Pendleton said, in an understanding tone. "We could charge out and take them quickly. Though my own inclination is to let the dinosaurs thin the herd out a bit more."

Before the men could protest, as he was expecting, Pendleton pushed on, using his oratorial skills to silence the men.

"If we mount up and go in guns blazing, what will happen? That's right, they will decimate us. Not by the prey, but because we blundered into territory we know better than to enter." His eyes scanned the room, and he saw acquiescence appear on the men's faces. A smile crept across his lips. "But that doesn't mean we have to sit back and do nothing!"

Finaughty rumbled, the sound reminding the group of the beginning of a lion's roar and he said, "It sounds exactly like that's what you want us to do, Charles."

Pendleton nodded. Even with his ruddy cheeks, the older man was still a force to reckon with.

"True," Charles Roy Pendleton said softly, before raising his voice. "Gentlemen, what I'm suggesting is to continue what we've already been doing. This is a different type of prey; one we've not encountered before and I couldn't live with myself if something happened to you fine men. So, to make things more interesting, if after twelve hours they haven't been decimated, we'll go out."

Another cheer erupted from the men. Even the one on the floor mumbled his agreement, and Pendleton grinned. It was all going according to plan.

"And to sweeten the pot," he added, "I'll match any wager, plus an extra twenty percent. How's that for a good time?"

CHAPTER TWENTY-FIVE

Ahead of him, Sean Marshall finally saw the others. They were standing still and talking amongst each other. Seeing this, he blinked and shook his head; did they forget about the charging dinosaur or did something else distract them?

To his right, he heard a howling laugh and turning, he saw Oleg Bekmambetov crashing towards him. The Russian's eyes were wide with terror and the smile on his face made it clear he was happy to see Marshall.

"My friend! Help Oleg and he won't feed you to monsters," Bekmambetov said the moment he was within earshot.

Shaking his head, Marshall glanced behind him. The Ankylosaurus was still there, and gaining but it was tired. Its breathing seemed laboured, yet it was keeping the same pace as before and the eyes were unfocused.

The animal wasn't used to keeping up such a constant speed.

Turning back, Marshall lifted the MP5 and using his thumb, switched the rate of fire to single shot. The moment he heard the click, his finger pressed down, squeezing the trigger, and a single shot cracked.

Ahead, he saw the others stop, then turn. Dillahunt smiled before pointing at him, acting like he'd spotted a friend across the street.

"Fucking move!" Marshall shouted, then pointed at the charging dinosaur. "Keep going!"

Hearing his words, then seeing the Ankylosaurus behind him, Dillahunt nodded, turned, then ran through the trees, using his arms to part them. As he did, a shaft of bright sunlight cut through the dinginess of the jungle, and Marshall smiled.

There was something else out there.

"Will you help me, friend little man?" Bekmambetov asked again and looking, Marshall saw genuine fear on his face.

Nodding, Marshall turned and fired again. He didn't care about killing the dinosaur, to do that he needed heavy ordinance. All he was trying to do was slow it down even more. That way, he'd have time to figure out what to do in their new surroundings.

Preparing himself, he and the Russian crashed through the tree line and into bright, warm light.

Covering his eyes, it took Marshall a second to blink away the glare and the blinding white of the sun. The moment he could see again, a smile formed.

He could work with this.

A large plain unfolded as far as they could see. It was beautiful and reminded Marshall of a wheat field in the middle of summer. Above him, the sky was clear except for a few clouds and a gentle breeze that cooled his face.

"Move!"

The Russian's voice snapped him out of his reverie and Marshall moved towards the others. They were already two hundred metres away from the jungle and waiting for the stragglers.

Getting closer, Marshall glanced down and his smile grew. Long blades of grass rubbed against his waist and looking about, he felt like he was in the middle of a green lake. Without realising it, he laughed, feeling safe and ready to take on the world again.

Seeing the others' startled expressions, Marshall gestured at the Russian and said, "It followed me home."

"You're not keeping it," Dillahunt snapped before the Ankylosaurus' bellow silenced him. Swallowing, the Southerner patted Marshall's shoulder, pointed and said, "Any other bright ideas?"

Turning around, the Irishman's mouth dropped open. He couldn't believe the sheer destructive power on display as the dinosaur exploded through the trees; the large sturdy trunks bent like saplings, birds cried out and took flight as their homes were destroyed and the moment each tree hit their breaking point, loud cracks and snaps filled the air.

The terrifying thing, though, was the fact that the Ankylosaurus didn't even notice the trees. Its gaze was solely on the group and it snorted in anger.

Watching it, Marshall said, "We need to split up. Two groups. If we confuse it, then I can get in close enough and put that thing down easily." It wasn't the best plan, but the only one he could think of. As long as the others followed his orders, there was a slim chance it would work.

"*No es tiempo de morir*," Alvaradejo said in Spanish before shrugging then cracking her neck.

"What did you say?" Marshall asked as he checked the magazine. So far, he had only fired the one shot which left him another twenty-nine rounds. Not including the one already loaded.

"She said, no time like the present to die," Dillahunt said before nodding and stretching. He looked at the still surprised faces of the others and grunted. "Yes, the redneck hillbilly can speak Spanish. Let's move on," he said before gesturing at the dinosaur.

Turning to face it, Marshall saw the dino paw at the ground, readying to charge again. He'd have one chance to take it down, and if he didn't time it perfectly, they'd be as dead as Hoskins.

"On my mark," he said, adjusting his grip on the weapon, "head left as fast as you can. The others go right. Zig-zag and go two hundred paces before meeting in the middle of the field."

"What about you, Seamus?"

"I'll do what I can."

Behind him, Dillahunt laughed, then held out his hand. Glancing at it, then to the man's face, Marshall raised a questioning eyebrow. "You're not going to make it on your own. Hand over the SIG."

"Fine," Marshall said as he handed the holster, gun, and spare magazines over. He watched as the other man expertly inspected the weapon; he tested the slide before making sure the magazine was fully loaded, then looked down the sight.

"Do me a favour," Marshall said as Dillahunt clipped the holster to his belt and stuffed the spare magazines into his pockets. "Don't shoot me in the back. Okay?"

All Walter Dillahunt did in answer was give a cheeky smile before saying in a pitch-perfect Elvis impression, "T.C.B, baby. Always taking care of business."

CHAPTER TWENTY-SIX

Before Marshall could respond, the Southerner took off, jogging towards the Ankylosaurus, oblivious to the difference in size and firepower. That's how it looked to Marshall, but he was quickly learning not to underestimate Dillahunt.

"Split up. Now!" Marshall barked at the others before following the other man. He moved fast, trying to catch-up. He suspected Dillahunt would be dead without his help, or mangled beyond recognition.

Ahead of them, the dinosaur shook its head at the sight of two men approaching it. The low rumbling started again before turning into a bellow that made them hesitate.

Seeing the momentary pause, the Ankylosaurus bounded forward, launching itself into a gallop. Its head lowered; it was clear its target was the two men.

"What's the plan, then?"

Marshall took a breath before flipping the MP5's firing rate to semi-auto. It was a good question and in fact he didn't have a concrete plan except buying the others enough time to get away.

"Seamus! Stay with me, son. This is your party."

"Shut up," Marshall said as he held the rifle tight. "Just do whatever you can to slow it down. We're not going to kill it with these."

Dillahunt snorted, flipping the P239's safety off. "Not with that attitude we won't," he said before swallowing. Beads of sweat formed on his forehead and the man looked ready to turn tail and follow the others. "Let's kill this Fuckofasaurus."

Hearing the made-up name, Marshall laughed as an idea came to him. "This is what we'll do. I'll slow it down. Nobody likes getting a faceful—"

"Phrasing."

"Focus, will ya?" Marshall said, judging the distance between them and the still charging dinosaur. It wasn't running as fast as before, and the tiny eyes darted about, like it was searching for something. Maybe it was making sure nobody else was going to attack? That was silly, he reasoned, it was a fucking dinosaur.

"Yes, Seamus. Do continue with your masterful plan as the Fuckofasaurus gets closer."

Dillahunt was right and if Marshall didn't put his plan into action soon, they'd be fucked. "Just follow my lead."

As the other man opened his mouth to answer, Marshall squeezed the trigger. The MP5 kicked as it spewed bullets, and both men watched the dinosaur lower its head, using the armour plating to deflect the tiny biting chunks of lead.

Seeing this, Marshall dropped to a knee and fired again.

Blood spurted from the animal's brow, and it shrieked in pain. Rearing back, Marshall saw crimson flow from the unprotected tissue, blinding the dinosaur perfectly

"Now!" he shouted and took off at a full run. He didn't bother looking behind him. Either Dillahunt kept up or he didn't. The plan was working and he couldn't waste time waiting for the other man to catch up.

Covering the distance quickly, Marshall squeezed the trigger in short bursts. Even though the gun was set to semi-automatic firing, he wanted to have as much control as possible. He didn't want to run out of ammunition in case they came up against something more dangerous.

Next to him, he heard Dillahunt's feet pounding the earth. "You're one crazy sumbitch, Seamus!"

"Try to get in my pants later," Marshall shouted back. It was hard to be heard over the cries of pain and anger from the dinosaur. "Right now, just focus on scaring that thing off. Do that and we can skip the foreplay."

Firing again, Marshall watched the dinosaur stop. It kept its head low, but the way the nostrils flared and its breathing became heavy made Marshall feel something was wrong.

Next to him, Dillahunt raised the pistol and started firing. His aim was slightly better than Marshall's. The 9mm bullets wouldn't do much to the large thick-skinned dinosaur.

"Fuck yeah!" Dillahunt crowed as the Ankylosaurus' left eye exploded in a fountain of blood and ocular goop.

The dinosaur shrieked, the sound filled with rage, pain and desperation. As the two men watched, the Ankylosaurus smashed its face into the dirt. It pushed forward, trying to soothe the damage done to its eye.

"What now, hoss?"

Marshall didn't know. He was too focused on the feeling of dread creeping up his spine. The last time he felt it that strong was just before an IED took out the majority of his old squad. This was different, the feeling was more primal, as if his entire body wanted to flee.

As he opened his mouth, a piss-inducing scream filled the air.

Spinning, both men held their weapons at the ready. The sound echoed, slowly fading, but Marshall knew what it was. The scream wasn't human at all. It belonged to an animal, one filled with hunger and a lust for blood.

"Seamus," Dillahunt said, his voice small and filled with fear. "What the fuck was that?"

Before he could answer, another of the inhuman sounds answered. This time it sounded like coughing, but there was an almost human-like chuckle to it. There was more than one out there, and they were communicating.

"No idea," Marshall said, turning back to the Ankylosaurus. The dinosaur looked about, its one remaining eye wide and full of fear. "But whatever it is, can't be good."

Dillahunt nodded, then asked, "Should we get back to the others?"

"Yep," Marshall said before a horrific snarling roar shattered the tension. "Fuck it, run!"

CHAPTER TWENTY-SEVEN

Heading for the others, Marshall heard the pounding of feet, the clicking of chattering teeth and the whooshing of bodies pushing through the grass. He didn't want to turn around. If he saw what was coming, he might lose his nerve.

"Don't look back," he said, more to himself than Dillahunt. Part of him was sure the other man wouldn't dare, but there was always blasted curiosity.

A panicked howl behind stopped them. It was stupid, but Marshall turned then immediately wished he hadn't. The sight was worse than anything he'd seen on the battlefield or could even imagine, yet there it was in bright technicolour.

There were five of them. Each was about two metres tall and charging towards the Ankylosaurus. It was hard to see them clearly, but the orange colouring and dark stripes running down the back and straight tails made them look like tigers. The fact they walked on two legs and extended their forearms out, ready to latch onto the petrified dinosaur, made them even more terrifying.

"That's disturbing," Dillahunt mumbled next to him, and Marshall nodded in agreement.

He knew what they were. It was obvious, but there was only one way to be one-hundred percent certain. The only problem was that he couldn't see the most defining feature of the fast-moving dinosaurs.

Then, almost as one, they launched themselves at the Ankylosaurus. Sailing through the air, the dinos shrieked triumphantly. The sound made Marshall's knees tremble, and instead of giving in to his fear, he watched the monsters.

On each foot, the dinos had a long-curved claw that reminded him of a cutthroat razor, and Marshall softly uttered their name. "Raptors."

"No fucking way," Dillahunt said, shaking his head rapidly. "Those things are Death Turkeys. That's all. Mutated turkeys."

Not bothering to look at him, Marshall ejected the magazine and checked the bullet counter on its side. There were two bullets left, not worth firing, then having to reload. Grunting, he tossed the useless magazine away, then quickly loaded a fresh one as the Ankylosaurus cried out.

Looking up, both men saw the raptors, one by one, latch onto the dinosaur. The instant their front claws grasped the thick hide, the curved toe-claw began its work. Cutting deeply with each kick, the raptors' aim was to slice open their target, then stick their long, pointed snouts into the wounds and feast.

As they attacked the herbivore, the Ankylosaurus bucked wildly, doing all it could to dislodge the smaller dinosaurs. All it did was make the raptors dig their claws in deeper.

It amazed Marshall how the raptors worked as a unit. They chatted to each other, making different sounds depending on what they needed done. *A perfect squad*, he thought before movement caught his eyes.

Turning, he spotted another raptor creeping through the grass. Only its tail was visible, cutting the air as it moved and every few feet it looked up before ducking down and continuing towards the rest of its hunting party.

"What the fuck is it up to?"

"Don't know. Don't care. Don't want to be here," Dillahunt answered while tugging on Marshall's sleeve. "Let's boogie, hoss. Those things spot us and we're dead."

He was right, and Marshall knew it. The more time they wasted watching the raptors, the greater the chance of them being spotted, and he was positive that there was no way they'd be able to outrun the raptors.

"Double time it," Marshall said, shoving Dillahunt forward. Watching him run, Marshall made sure his weapon was fastened to his vest. He couldn't afford to lose it.

The shriek of an animal being tortured made him turn, and he gasped.

Clawing at the Ankylosaurus' face, the other raptor's toe-claws scratched at the herbivore's eye while its jagged tooth-filled mouth tore strips of flesh from its face.

Blood dribbled from the fresh, ugly wounds, pooling below the poor dinosaur.

Shaking his head, Marshall turned away and started after Dillahunt. If the raptors saw him, he needed a contingency to guarantee he and at least Dillahunt made it out safely.

Of course, he reminded himself, there was still the unknown factor called Pendleton.

Putting plenty of distance between him and the feeding raptors, Marshall saw Dillahunt spin, then bring up his pistol. His stance was good, but Marshall could make it perfect. *In another life*, he thought as he waved his hands at him, signalling Dillahunt to keep moving.

Then he heard it. Coming from both his left and right. It was the snarls and the coughing sound of more raptors!

Bringing up the MP5, Marshall readied himself to fire at the monsters. It would buy some time, but he was already down two magazines with only another three left and he didn't know how many rounds it'd take to put these deadly dinosaurs down.

"Get them moving!" he bellowed at Dillahunt as he turned to his left, lifted the rifle, and squeezed the trigger.

CHAPTER TWENTY-EIGHT

The barrel glowed as Marshal squeezed the trigger. He held it for two seconds before releasing and adjusting his aim and grip. Each magazine held thirty rounds, and he kept that number in his mind and decreased it with each burst of gunfire.

There were another five raptors, three to his left, with the remaining two on his right. Unfortunately, he couldn't focus on one side over the other. That would leave him wide open to an attack.

A shriek of pain followed by red mist came from the nearest raptor on his left and he smiled as the dinosaur slowed. Quickly, Marshall turned to his right and fired again, hoping for the same result.

Bullets slammed into the raptor's chest, shredding the scaly flesh easily. The dinosaur screamed, stumbled, then sped up, leaving an expanding trail of blood behind it.

With a snarl, the other raptor took the lead, hissing at Marshall.

"Yeah, fuck you too!" he shouted before turning to the front.

Ahead of him, he saw Dillahunt and the others running further into the grass. It made sense, but as they did, Marshall spotted tails heading towards them and it reminded him of the shark from *Jaws*.

Fuck! he thought as a shadowy form sped towards him.

Diving to the ground, Marshall rolled onto his back as the raptor's curved claws dug into the dirt. Squeezing the trigger, Marshall watched the dinosaur's face become nothing more than a pulpy mess.

Blood splattered his face and he spat, ridding himself of the vile liquid.

Half, Marshall thought, still keeping count of the bullets. Another four bursts, then he'd have to reload and that would be the perfect moment for the dinos to get him.

To his right, he heard a snarl and fired without thinking. A howl of pain sounded, followed by fleeing feet. Marshall smiled before scrambling to his feet, hoping the other raptors weren't still focused on him.

Scanning the area, he couldn't see tails or heads bobbing and weaving through the grass. That was good, but also bad. Without knowing the positions of the enemy, it would be impossible to prepare for an attack.

"Doesn't matter," he said to himself as he took off again, running towards the others. "Get to them and make sure they're safe. That's the priority."

It made sense now. The field was the raptor's hunting grounds, and he'd led the group right to them.

Marshall felt stupid as he got closer to the others. They were moving as one; backs pressed against each other, they performed a circular movement, keeping every angle in view. It was smart, but also slowed them down too much.

Some leader you are, he thought before shouting, "Move ya fucking asses! Now!"

Hearing his voice, Dillahunt and Tanaka looked at him. The Yakuza nodded, then stepped out of the circle and lifted a jagged branch. He held it like a sword, ready to slice at any who got too close.

Dillahunt, on the other hand, lifted his gun, said something to the others then squeezed the trigger.

A single gunshot rang clear, and as the group scattered, all heading in the same direction but individually, the raptors lifted their heads to see what the disturbance was.

The pistol dropped, and Dillahunt fired at the closest raptor. With a squeal, the dinosaur vanished. The rest bellowed their disapproval before bounding towards the group of fleeing humans.

Squeezing the trigger, Marshall did what he could to steer the charging raptors away from the group. His aim wasn't the best. He needed to rest and rehydrate, but he was steady enough to hit something.

Leading the target, he waited for the opportune time to fire, and smiled whenever a red mist appeared, or the raptor yelped, and disappeared.

The moment his gun clicked empty, Marshall ejected the spent magazine and slammed a fresh one into the sub-machine gun. As soon as he felt it lock into place, he yanked back on the slide, aimed, then fired again.

He knew, though, as he caught up to the others, that he'd run out of ammunition. The moment that happened, if they weren't out of the raptors' territory, they'd be eviscerated and their bloody remains feasted on.

"How many you got left?" he said to Dillahunt the moment he joined the group. He turned and fired at another raptor. They were coming from everywhere now, and he found it hard to keep track of their numbers. He counted about twenty-five, not including the ones he'd taken out, but it was impossible to be certain of their numbers.

Dillahunt grunted then used a sleeve to wipe sweat from his eyes. "Not enough," he said and his voice and expression made it clear that the old Delta Force operator was still kicking about inside. "You got a Hail Mary save our asses plan, Seamus? Now's the time to pull it out of your ass."

He was right. Unfortunately, Marshall didn't have any idea what they were going to do. The deeper they went, the more the raptors charged. It didn't make any sense—

One of the others, a man, bellowed in terror. He spun, and just before he fell to the ground, all saw the raptor clawing away at his stomach. The front claws curved around his sides, penetrating his lungs while the jaws crushed, then chewed on the poor soul's face.

Blood stained the grass as Marshall shouted, "Don't fucking stop! Whatever you do, don't fucking stop!"

CHAPTER TWENTY-NINE

Moving as fast as they could, Marshall and Dillahunt did all they could to keep the front and rear of the group clear of the ferocious monsters.

That's what the raptors were. There was nothing natural about the way they looked, moved, sounded, or attacked.

"Hey, Seamus," Dillahunt called as he fired at another raptor. The dino leapt away, then hissed at him before spinning and vanishing into the grass. "You got any other weapons?"

Squeezing the trigger again, Marshall watched one of the creatures fall to the ground. It twitched, then went still. Not wanting to risk it attacking later, the Irishman lifted the rifle, and squeezed the trigger.

The bullets tore through the raptor's cranium; it shrieked in pain before going silent.

"Fuckers know how to play possum," Marshall called, then squeezed the trigger again. The weapon clicked, and he swore. If he was going to reload, he'd need someone to cover him. "Joe!"

To his right, he heard a high-pitched wail of terror, followed by a wet crunch. Turning, Marshall saw the jaws of a raptor wrapped around another man's throat. The yellow-ish eye stared at him, then with a sharp twisting motion, it snapped the neck.

As the body went limp, the dinosaur dragged it into the grass.

They were being picked off quicker than he expected, and Marshall's mind drew blanks as far as how they were going to get away from the dinosaurs.

"Where the fuck's Tanaka?" he heard himself say as a screaming raptor launched itself at him. Flipping the rifle so he held it by the barrel, Marshall swung hard. His arms vibrated from the impact and he watched the dinosaur collapse.

"He's helping me!" Dillahunt grunted.

Just perfect, Marshall thought as he ejected the spent magazine. Fumbling to load another, he felt a hulking form stand next to him. Flinching, he looked up and saw the Russian.

"I help," Bekmambetov said before lifting his leg high above the unconscious dinosaur. "Stand back," he added before gritting his teeth and stomping the raptor's head.

The ground shook from the impact and the cracking of bones filled the air, snapping, then a slight pop as the dino's cranium caved in.

Blinking away his shock, Marshall finished loading the weapon. He lifted it and fired at another raptor, missing this time, and it sounded like the animal laughed.

"Thanks," he said as an idea formed. It was crazy enough to work, but they'd lose more men than he was willing to. The alternative, though, was the utter annihilation of them all, and Pendleton would win.

"Frederica," Marshall said while the Russian stood ready. The giant's arms hung by his sides and he swayed slightly, ready to attack any monster that came too close. "Frederica," he repeated until he felt a slap on his shoulder.

Turning his head, he saw the Mexican. Marshall smiled at the sight of her holding two jagged jaw bones as if they were blades. She was ready and the moment a raptor charged her, she swiped down then up.

The dinosaur stumbled back, shaking its head, trying to find what attacked it. Large, ugly gashes cut its snout and the raptor turned, whimpering, and fled.

A scream caught his attention, and spinning to his right, Marshall fired again. But he was too slow this time and two raptors dodged the bullets easily before leaping over him and Bekmambetov.

The Russian caught one by its tail and strained, pulling it backwards, making the dinosaur yelp in surprise. As he did, the giant swung the dinosaur above his head before slamming it into the ground.

Spinning, Marshall brought up the MP5 and trained it on the other raptor. His eyes widened as he watched the monster bring up one of its feet and spin.

He didn't have time to call out, and even if he did, it wouldn't have done anything. The raptor was too fast, its target too slow.

The dinosaur growled as it finished spinning and the man bellowed in pain and gripped his belly. Blood poured from the fresh wound; his hands covered in crimson. As he screamed, he coughed, and his intestines slipped out from between his fingers.

Seeing its winnings, the raptor howled before jumping on top of the man. Its weight did the trick, and they slammed into the ground.

Before Marshall could squeeze the trigger, Joe Tanaka appeared. Blood covered his face and clothes, his shirt already brown from the drying liquid, and he raised the makeshift sword high and shifted his weight.

His foot cracked a twig, startling the raptor, who looked up. Pieces of viscera hung from its jaws and it hissed at the Yakuza.

Ignoring the sight and sound, Tanaka brought the sharpened branch down at a steep angle. His movement was faster than anything Marshall had seen. He didn't see the moment it made contact with the raptor's flesh.

He did see the results.

The raptor flinched, both eyes rolling up in its head as its mouth hung open. A slither of blood trickled along a thick line and with a gasp, the dinosaur flopped to the ground. Dead.

Slicing the air, Tanaka cleaned the blade, then turned, raised it above his head, ready to dispatch another.

They were down to five now, including Marshall, and looking at the group, he finally felt as if they had a chance to bring down Pendleton and escape the island. Not even the raptors seemed as big a problem as before.

Squeezing the trigger, the gun clicked empty again.

Shit, Marshall thought before shouting, "Reloading. This is my last magazine."

"I'm already out," Dillahunt said a second before throwing the empty P239 pistol at one of the dinosaurs.

The gun passed the raptor easily, and it lunged for him. Luckily, Tanaka stepped in the way and disposed of the animal with an elegant flourish.

Blood spurted from the dead animal's neck, covering both men and the ground in crimson.

"Form up," Marshall said as he yanked on the slide. He needed to make each shot count, while also figuring out what to do once he ran out of bullets. "Make sure these cunts don't make it through again."

He felt Bekmambetov's body slam against his right side a second before Alvaradejo's slim frame crashed into his left side. The woman grunted, then flicked her hair. She didn't make eye contact with him, being too focused on not getting killed.

He felt the other two bodies press against his back and Dillahunt asked, "You ready to pull a miracle out of your ass yet, Seamus?"

"Working on it," Marshall said as more raptors emerged from the grass. They moved slowly, wary of the group, and Marshall smiled. He knew they were going to surround them and the moment that happened, they'd attack.

Until then, they still had time for a miracle to happen.

Sighing softly as he prepared to fire, Sean Marshall softly said, "Working on it."

CHAPTER THIRTY

The sound of glass breaking filled the area, making both human and raptor look about in confusion. Another shattering of glass sounded, followed by two more, and Marshall frowned.

Looking up, he gagged, fighting the urge to throw up. Never in his life had Marshall smelt something so foul. The stench of decomposing bodies, left out in the scorching sun, bloated, was as sweet as roses compared to this, and his eyes watered.

Marshall blinked, trying to clear them, then looked at the others. Each were gagging, dry retching as the odour assaulted their sinuses and, for a moment, he wondered if this was the attack of a prehistoric skunk.

A whimper caught his attention, and taking his eyes off the others, he saw the raptors. The dinosaurs scratched their snouts, trying to rid themselves of the rancid smell. Their claws dug into the flesh and trails of blood formed.

One of the raptors shrieked before backing away from the group. It lowered itself to the ground, letting the grass soothe itself.

Forgetting himself, Marshall breathed deeply and almost lost control of his stomach. His diaphragm heaved, spasming from the stench, and he covered his mouth and nose with his arm.

"Gawddamn," Dillahunt gasped as he tore a strip of material from his shirt. "This is worse than bear spray!"

On Marshall's other side, Bekmambetov grunted, then shook his head. "Nothing natural made this. It burns!"

The Russian was right about that and seeing the Southerner wrap the tattered cloth around his face, Marshall followed suit. The moment he tied it tightly at the back of his head, he immediately breathed easier.

"We need to move," he said, though it was impossible to know if the others heard him. The cries of the raptors drowned him out and, staring at the dinos, Marshall could see they weren't in pain, but afraid.

What the fuck is going on? The thought barely left his head when one of the raptors, tired of the offensive smell, spun then disappeared from view, cutting a trail through the grass.

"Down!" Marshall signalled for the others to drop. He didn't wait for them to follow his order. There was something familiar about the situation and his training told him to stay low to the ground.

At least for now.

Watching the others lie flat on the blood-soaked ground, Marshall crawled towards them.

"That's some plan, Seamus," Dillahunt chuckled, then coughed. "What's next? You going to make the Statue of Liberty appear? Or maybe walk through the Great Wall of China? Sorry, Joey, not sure if that's insensitive to you lot."

Tanaka ignored the remark. Tilting his head to the side, he held up his hand, silencing the other man before he could say anything else.

"I said sorry," Dillahunt mumbled before lifting his head. "Anyone else hear that whistling?"

It took Marshall a second to focus in on it. The raptors' terrified shrieks and snarls made it almost impossible to detect anything else, but the moment he found it, it was all he could hear. A high-pitched whistle, like a nerf dart, grew louder with each second. Almost like it was—

"Incoming!" Marshall bellowed, using his arms to protect his head.

An instant later, a dull thud sounded, followed by another and another. His instincts told him to expect explosions, the sounds reminding him of grenades hitting the ground.

If they were explosives, then the entire area would be destroyed.

Instead of the roar and flash of fire from a frag grenade, Marshall heard a hiss, then smelt smoke. Opening his eyes, he saw plumes of thick grey smoke rise from between blades of grass, covering the area in a thick blanket.

Someone was helping them.

Pushing himself off the ground, Marshall kept below the top of the grass. It was a precaution in case whoever was providing them cover was one of Pendleton's men. If that was the case, then it'd be folly to give him clear targets.

But then, Marshall thought as he watched the raptors look about, confusion and fear mixing in their wild eyes, *if it was one of the lunatics, why would they even bother using smoke grenades?*

Before they could find an answer, the dinosaurs chattered, the sound high-pitched and frantic. Then as one, they turned, running through the grass back to their nests and safety from the smoke and horrid smell.

"What the fuck is going on?" Marshall asked, waving the smoke away. He didn't want to completely displace the stuff. That would give whoever was out there a clear shot. But he needed to see what was out there.

To his right he felt another presence and, turning, saw Dillahunt. "Someone up there likes you."

About time, Marshall thought as he scanned the horizon. To the right was the jungle. In the fight and retreat, they'd gotten turned around. The raptors knew exactly what they were doing, and he nodded, impressed with their abilities.

Further ahead of them, the field became rolling hills, and the grass disappeared over the first crest, leaving his mind to ponder what was on the other side.

"*No estamos solos*," Alvaradejo said, tapping Marshall's shoulder. He followed her extended hand and took a step forward.

Standing next to a large gnarled tree, it reminded him of a baobab tree, stood a lone figure. It was hard to make him out properly, but all Marshall could tell was they didn't look threatening.

"What's he doing?" Dillahunt asked.

The Russian stood in front of the group, lifted his hand to block the sun from his eyes, then said after a second of studying the figure, "He's letting us know he's no threat."

That made sense and Marshall felt a wave of relief wash over him, followed by a series of questions, and he felt the urge to approach the figure. But there was a part of him that knew it wasn't a good idea. There was always the possibility that this was a ruse designed to lure them into a false sense of security.

"What's the play, Seamus?"

Hearing Dillahunt's voice, Marshall blinked, then smiled behind the fabric covering his mouth and nose.

The figure jogged towards them. With each passing second, he sped up, getting closer to them. A tattered piece of fabric covered his body, acting like a poncho, patches sewn roughly held it together.

Large goggles covered the figure's eyes and as it neared them, instead of slowing down, it sped up and said, "Follow me, now!"

It took Marshall a second to register the command. He couldn't believe the voice was female!

CHAPTER THIRTY-ONE

"How'd you scare off the raptors? What's your name?" Marshall asked the stranger. He found it hard to keep up with her, she moved easily through the jungle and kept a fast pace. Obviously, she wanted to get as far away from the raptors as possible.

Trying to get her to interact, he asked, "That's not the first time you've done that, right?"

The woman shook her head, then, moving again, said, "You made me use the last of my bombs and ultimate deterrent. So, forgive me if I'm not leaping at the chance to make friends with you, Irish."

Shaking his head, Marshall turned back and focused on the woman leading them. Her attitude wasn't that of a killer, nor anyone with training, but the way she moved through the foliage, it was clear she knew what she was doing. The only questions were, how long had she been on the island? What was her story? And most importantly, did she know how to get to Pendleton?

"You didn't have to save us," he said before going silent. It sounded childish, but he needed her to engage with them properly. It was all well and good for her to lead them about, but if they were to walk in silence, he wouldn't trust her.

"I did," the woman said with a heavy sigh. "I saw how you handled the Ankylosaurus and steggie. If anyone can... Well, it made sense at the time. Besides," she said, chuckling, "it'd be nice to have some company that isn't going to get killed quickly."

"Love the vote of confidence," Dillahunt said from behind the two. "What's your name, darling? If you don't have one, I'll be glad to get to know you and find a fitting moniker for you."

"Not darling, that's for sure," the woman said, slowing down. "Call me Haywood," she said with a curt nod to the others. "Don't worry about first names. Out here, they're not important. What is, is surviving. So, follow me and keep the idiotic questions to yourselves."

The sound of running water filled the air and sniffing, Marshall smelt the sweet aroma of a freshwater stream. He smiled and quickened his pace, the memory of his grandparents' place propelling him.

Behind him, he heard the others scrambling after him, but it didn't matter. He sensed that the way ahead was clear.

Breaking through a thicket of vines and leaves, Marshall sighed while his face split into an even bigger grin.

It was picture perfect. A river cut the land, but the flowers and trees that bloomed near it looked like something out of a fantasy world. Shafts of light cut through the jungle's canopy, giving everything a serene ambience, and Marshall felt as if he was back in Ireland.

"Wow," Tanaka gasped, and Marshall chuckled. The sight was unexpected, but after the bloodshed and constant running for their lives, they appreciated the sight.

"Keep moving," Haywood said, stepping in front of the five awe-filled people. "You can drink and clean any wounds, but you don't want to stand still for too long. Every inch of this place is dangerous."

As they walked, following the river, Marshall watched each of the others bend down, scoop up a handful of water and drink. Alvaradejo splashed water on her face, wincing as the cool liquid cleaned the gash on her forehead.

"It doesn't seem dangerous for you," Marshall said, slowly easing into debriefing the woman. "You know how to move and what to do. You been here long?"

Haywood shrugged and grunted a non-committal answer. Lowering her poncho's hood, Marshall saw flowing red hair that was matted and in need of washing. Still walking, she removed the facemask, then her goggles, and sighed.

"When you were up there," she said, pointing to the sky, "did they spray you with anything?"

Marshall blinked before turning to the others. It was a strange question to ask, but it felt important and as he remembered everything that happened on the plane, Tanaka spoke.

"Yes. Before they dropped us, we passed through a haze."

Snapping his fingers, Dillahunt said, "I thought that was to cover the stench of the Russian. No offense, big hoss."

Bekmambetov didn't react to the insult. He was too focused on Haywood's face, and it was clear he was attracted to her. Marshall shook his head. If he tried anything, it'd be hell to stop him and that was a worry.

"That wasn't a wash or disinfectant. In fact, it was quite the opposite," Haywood said with the tone of a reporter. "It's the same principle I used to save your asses, and what all life does to attract or repel mates, food, what have you. Pheromones."

Marshall raised a suspicious eyebrow. "Go on."

"I used T-Rex piss to scare—"

"They have a T-Rex?" Marshall asked as his childhood love for dinosaurs bubbled to the surface. Until now he'd been able to control it, but hearing that his all-time favourite was somewhere on the island, he smiled, giddy with happiness.

Haywood shook her head. "Everyone has that reaction until they see it up close. It's a monster, like all the dinosaurs," she said, her voice soft and serious.

"What's a T-Rex?" Dillahunt asked. He looked at the others, confusion and annoyance on his face as he tried to keep up with the conversation. "Don't leave me out in the dark, people. What's a fucking T-Rex?"

Even the Russian couldn't believe what he was hearing. The giant placed a hand on Dillahunt's shoulder, almost driving him to the ground, and asked, "Don't you know dinosaurs?"

"No. I was busy living my life."

"It's a tyrannosaurus rex," Marshall said slowly, making himself heard as if he was talking to a struggling student. "The king of the dinosaurs?"

Dillahunt shook his head. It was clear he didn't know what they were talking about, and Marshall decided not to describe the king of the dinosaurs. Instead, he said, "It's big with large jaws and can eat you in one go."

"Oh," Dillahunt said with a nod. "You mean a Shityourpantsasaurus."

"You've got to be fucking kidding," Haywood said, pinching the bridge of her nose tight. "I should've let the raptors eat you."

Turning to face the woman, Marshall said, "You didn't, which means you want off the island. You help us and we'll get you home safe and sound. My word on it."

He didn't see the woman's face. Haywood turned before she answered and started walking again. "Pendleton uses custom-made pheromones to make sure the dinosaurs, even the herbivores, go crazy and attack whoever they smell. I don't know how he did it. The T-Rex piss does the trick of keeping them at bay. But I've run out of the stuff because of you."

Walking in silence, Marshall's mind processed the new information. It made sense that their gracious host would cheat, anything to guarantee winning, and that the easiest way to do so was using the dinosaurs.

But the question remained, how would they get around the problem of the pheromones?

"Have you found a way to get rid of them?"

Haywood shook her head before speaking. "You think I'd still be here if I did? Get your head out of your ass, soldier-boy. Nothing's normal here," she said before pointing at their surroundings. "We're in the middle of some Skull Island bullshit. Normal doesn't exist here anymore."

She had a valid point and as they trudged along, Marshall's mind twisted and turned, trying to figure out a way to rid themselves of the chemical mixture that drove the dinos crazy.

"Feel free to speak up," he said, turning to look at the others. They'd kept out of the conversation, but now he needed their opinions and thoughts. Even the most stupid suggestion could lead to a piece of brilliant thinking.

Dillahunt coughed, exaggerating the sound until Marshall acknowledged him. Smiling like a kid who had the greatest idea in the world, he said, "I know a way."

CHAPTER THIRTY-TWO

Before Marshall could bombard him with questions, Dillahunt turned and faced the water. He took a breath, rolled his shoulders like he was prepping for a fight, then took a step towards the riverbank.

"Wait," Bekmambetov rumbled, using a solid hand to stop the smaller man. "What is plan?"

"Well, it's simple," the Southerner said, removing the slab of meat called a hand from his shoulder. "If I understand it properly, we've been doused in some chemical that makes the monsters, not dinos," he said pointedly at Marshall, "go apeshit. So, all we need to do is wash it off."

Marshall closed his eyes, taking a moment to compose himself. It was so simple and, in a way, innocent, that a part of him hoped it would work. Glancing at Haywood, he saw her cover her grinning mouth.

"You come up with that all by yourself?"

"*Vas a morir, coño,*" Alvaradejo said. She crossed her arms and stood with a disapproving look on her face.

Looking at the Mexican, Dillahunt pouted, then said, "You don't know that for sure, sweet cheeks. What's with all the negative attitude?"

It was clear the man wasn't going to be dissuaded from his course of action, and seeing this, Marshall nodded. He wasn't their commanding officer, or even their leader, yet he was acting like it. That wasn't strange. What was, was the fact they were following him. Extreme circumstances made strange bedfellows.

"You're too kind, fearless leader," Dillahunt said with a low bow. He winked at Haywood before turning to face the giant. "Out of my way, tiny."

Bekmambetov shook his head, folded his arms across his massive chest and widened his stance. "No," he growled. "You don't go. Too small a surface area. For real test, Oleg is perfect."

Before anyone could say anything, the Russian turned, took two gigantic steps, and slid into the water. His massive form barely disturbed the water's surface, and he vanished. All anyone could see was a shadowy form moving to the centre of the river.

"You know anything about water dinosaurs? Or other nasties living in the water?" Marshall asked Haywood, his eyes focused on the bubbles floating to the top of the water.

Next to him, the woman scratched her chin, then shook her head. "Never seen anything. But that doesn't mean there isn't any," she said, then went silent. Her eyes focused on the horizon, and Marshall knew she was remembering her past life.

"Seamus, a word?"

Hearing Dillahunt's voice, Marshall walked away from Haywood. He felt sorry for her but also immense admiration. It took a strength of will to not only survive but also thrive in the land of dinosaurs. A part of him wanted to wrap her up and protect her, but he knew that was his own upbringing coming into play.

"What is it?" he said. Dillahunt stood at the edge of the water, a long blade of grass in his hand that he played with absently. Not far from him were the others, Tanaka and Alvaradejo. The moment they saw him, they walked over.

"We wanted to apologise," Dillahunt said without any preamble. "What we did back there, it wasn't right and if we'd listened to you instead of each other—"

"More might be alive," Tanaka said, finishing the thought. His face was a blank mask, but his eyes sparkled with thanks. He spoke genuinely, his gratitude real, and the Irishman nodded.

"Even though it was your fault we ended up here," Dillahunt continued, and anger flashed across his face for a split second. "How were you to know this was the reason for the bounties on us, right?"

"Don't let it happen again," Alvaradejo said in almost perfect English. She turned and walked away, heading towards Haywood and leaving the others in stunned silence.

In the water, they heard a loud splash, followed by a gasp of breath. Turning, Marshall saw the Russian explode from the water like a whale breeching. He smiled at them before diving back under. It was clear he was enjoying himself immensely.

"Did you know she could speak English?" Dillahunt asked softly. "Her voice sounds amazing!"

Marshall shook his head. It was clear Walter Dillahunt was smitten by the cartel killer, and Marshall hoped he knew what he was doing.

"No idea. There was nothing in her file about it."

Dillahunt nodded, then shook his head. "Sorry, Seamus," he said sheepishly. "What were you saying?"

Smiling at the man, Marshall led him and the Yakuza back to the women.

"It doesn't matter how many of us are left," he said the moment they were close enough to Haywood and Alvaradejo. "The dinos aren't our biggest problem. Nor is it Pendleton and his band of merry lunatics."

"Share with the group, fearless leader," Haywood said.

"It's us," Marshall said. "If we don't work together as a team, we're not going to make it. No offence, Haywood, we can follow you anywhere, but without a plan of attack, we'll be dead sooner rather than later."

Dillahunt nodded, then said, "Well, I've got experience working like that. Though I might be a tad bit rusty."

"Don't look at me," Haywood said, stepping away from the others. "I'm not a soldier, or even a tactician." It was clear she was out of her depths, and if pushed, would probably shut down.

Marshall nodded and smiled reassuringly. "It won't matter," he said and the old ways of talking came back. "You know the lay of the land. That's all we need from you. The rest of us can handle Pendleton and his men. Get us to them, and we'll get you off the island.

"That's the plan," he said, looking at the others. "Take down Pendleton and get home. Sound good?"

CHAPTER THIRTY-THREE

"*Да*, it sounds good," the Russian said as he exited the water. He shook his head, running his fingers through his hair. Water droplets dribbled from him and if he wasn't covered in tattoos and blood, Bekmambetov might've passed for a model.

"That's the vote that counts," Dillahunt muttered with a chuckle. He went over to Bekmambetov and sniffed him. Frowning, he sniffed again before turning to face the others. "I can't smell shit. Anyone know what pheromones smell like?"

Instantly, Marshall turned to Haywood and waited for her to answer. If anyone knew, he reasoned, it was her.

"Pheromones are things you can't smell," the woman said after a few seconds' silence. "They work on a level our sinuses can't decipher, but we know when they affect us. Plus, they manufactured these for the dinosaurs, which have some of the biggest olfactory cavities of any species."

Dillahunt scratched his cheek and mumbled, "What the fuck's an olfactory?"

"It's what you smell with, *puto*," Alvaradejo said, shushing him.

Haywood nodded at the Mexican, then continued talking. "There's no way to know if your plan worked," she said, and her voice sounded like a teacher's. "It's highly probable that all you did was cover it for a few minutes. The bacteria and microbes living in the river would have their own smells and the dinosaurs would pick up on those."

"But," Marshall said, picking up her train of thought, "once you dried off, the original smell would reappear."

The red-haired woman nodded, then said to Dillahunt, "It's a good idea. But the only way to guarantee it worked would be to—"

"To approach a dinosaur and see if it attacked," Tanaka finished her sentence. It was a sobering thought, and everyone knew it was the only way to make sure Dillahunt's idea was a success. The question then became, what sort of dino to approach?

Alvaradejo spoke first. Her voice was soft, but full of confidence. "Is that why you never tried it?"

The other woman nodded, and her eyes filled with tears. "I'm a coward," she said, before turning away and rubbing her eyes. "It would've been easier if I had your skills, but I'm a science teacher specialising in chemistry and biology."

That explains her knowledge, Marshall thought as he made the hard decision. Turning to face the Russian giant, he said, "Nobody's going to make you do this, buddy. If you don't want to, fine. But we'll do all we can to make sure you don't die."

"Nothing can kill Oleg," Bekmambetov stated, talking over Marshall. He pounded his chest like a gorilla before saying, "The American D.E.A., Marshals, and O.C.U. came after me. Want to know where they are now? In hospital or ground. What that tell you about Oleg?"

That you're not as dangerous as you act, Marshall thought before answering. He needed to play this carefully, especially if they chose the wrong dinosaur. It could end badly.

"Whatever you say, Oleg," he said finally, before turning to the others. "Let's find our Russian bear here a playmate."

Behind him he heard Bekmambetov growl, or chuckle. It was hard to tell at times, and Marshall hoped Dillahunt's idea actually worked. The more he was around this group of thieves, criminals and killers, the more he felt at home.

"I saw that," Dillahunt chuckled next to him. "You like us now."

Using a grunt to cover his annoyance at being discovered, Marshall shoved the man, saying, "Make yourself useful!"

The Southerner chuckled as the group of six started moving. Their steps were soft, but sure-footed. None wanted to give away their position. The tension was palpable and each of them knew what the stakes were.

"There," Tanaka said, and gestured to the left of their position.

Stepping forward, Marshall squinted against the shafts of light. Twenty metres ahead, a large bush shook and he could hear soft grunts. Something was feeding.

"This will do," Bekmambetov said, pushing past the others. He strode with purpose towards the trembling fern. As he got closer, the grunting stopped, turning into a growl, which slowed his pace.

Dillahunt shook his head and whistled, impressed with the display. "That's one crazy sumbitch, I tell you what."

"You just did," Marshall said softly, focusing his attention on the man walking away from them. It was clear from the sounds that it wasn't the compies or even one of the larger herbivores. That was good, but if it was something else, another carnivore, then they'd be fucked.

"Come out and face me!" the Russian roared before picking up a stick and throwing it at the bush. His makeshift weapon pierced the plant, eliciting a startled yelp from whatever was behind it. Bekmambetov laughed as he saw the small dinosaur bounce out from its hiding spot.

Taller than a twelve-year-old boy, the dinosaur's beaked mouth made it clear it was a herbivore and the group sighed in relief. It stood on two legs, with the front ones curved under its chest, like the raptors. But what Marshall found interesting was the head.

Unlike the other dinos he'd seen, this one had a large domed top that looked like bone. Tiny ridges circled it, giving it the resemblance of a monk's haircut, and he chuckled. "What the fuck is that?"

"Pachycephalosaur," Haywood said, and backed away slightly. "You don't want that thing charging at you. It's fast and once that head locks in place, it's a juggernaut."

"It's cute!" Bekmambetov cooed at the dinosaur. He stepped towards it and held out a hand, showing he didn't mean it any harm.

Marshall watched as the dinosaur studied the approaching man. Its head swayed from side to side and it clicked and grunted.

It turned away from the Russian, and the others cheered. Dillahunt's idea had worked!

The sound of deep long sniffing filled the air and looking back at the pachycephalosaur, Marshall saw its raised head bobbing up and down.

Something was wrong.

Turning on its heels, the dinosaur focused on the Russian. It took another deep breath, then roared before charging at the man.

"Move it!" Marshall bellowed, but it was too late.

Lowering its head, the dinosaur's neck aligned, locking in place with a loud click. There was nothing Bekmambetov could do as the small animal sped up. In a few seconds, it was moving as fast as a cheetah.

"We need to go, now!" Haywood said as the pachycephalosaur's head connected with Bekmambetov's stomach.

The man was lifted off his feet, sailing through the air. His scream trailed after the others as they followed Haywood into the jungle, away from the river and the small dinosaur attacking the prone Russian's body.

Turning back, Marshall watched as the dinosaur brought its head down, smashing Oleg Bekmambetov's face into a pulpy bloody mess of blood, bone and mangled tissue.

Dillahunt's plan hadn't worked.

CHAPTER THIRTY-FOUR

"Is Friar Tuck going to follow us?" Dillahunt asked, looking back fervently. He stayed quiet as they ran through the bush, wet squelching mixed with the shattering of bones echoed after them. This was his first question since the death of the Russian.

Haywood shook her head and slowed. "No," she said, gasping for air. "The pachy can't keep that speed up for long. Besides, we're almost home." Stretching, she beckoned the others to follow her and said, "How the fuck are you able to run like that and not be dead?"

Behind him, Marshall heard Alvaradejo and Tanaka laugh. It was a good sign, and he was grateful to hear it. Following the woman, he let them pass him and he watched Dillahunt.

"You okay?"

"That's why I wanted to be the one to test it," the Southerner said with a small sigh. "Too many men have died because of me."

The moment he said it, Marshall understood Walter Dillahunt better. His sordid history made sense and all he could think to do was nod and squeeze the man's arm. "We've all been there," he said, then chuckled. "You have to admit, after his bragging, it was poetic justice."

Dillahunt chuckled, then said, "True. It would've been great to see the look on his face."

Laughing, the two men followed the others. Marshall knew what Dillahunt meant, and his last mission came back to him. It was a shit-show that resulted in his old squad being hospitalised or buried, and he carried that weight with him every single day.

"You two done bonding?" Haywood called as they caught up to the others. She stood between Tanaka and Alvaradejo, looking amused at the sight of the two men appearing like Doctor Livingstone. "Or would you like some pina coladas and a walk along the beach?"

Ignoring her, Marshall sniffed, then blinked. His eyes stung and the same stench that scared the raptors filled his nostrils. This time, though, it was far more potent, to the point that he felt queasy.

"Keep moving," the redhead said, pulling both men towards her. Behind her was an enormous, gnarled, ancient tree. "Once we cross the perimeter, you'll be fine."

Following her orders, the four hurried to keep up with her. One by one, they crossed an invisible line and slowly their eyes stopped watering and the horrid reeking odour vanished, leaving them to see the clearing properly.

"T-Rex piss?" Marshall asked as he used his sleeve to wipe his face.

Haywood nodded and smiled. "Best thing to keep the dinos away. That and some rex shit does the trick."

Amazed at the ingenuity, Marshall nodded, then looked around at his surroundings, and felt a strange mixture of peacefulness and tension.

The area reminded him of the jungle depicted in Disney's *Tarzan*. The greens looked surreal, but he knew they were real. Towering over them, the centre-most tree rose up and as Haywood brought them closer to it, Marshall saw the rusted decomposing remains of an airplane.

Cocking his head to the side, he tried to see more of the aircraft, and his mind raced. There were too many possibilities for it being there, and all made him feel sick to his stomach.

"That's home?" Dillahunt asked, then chuckled nervously. He stood next to Alvaradejo, who was trembling uncontrollably. Gently, he squeezed her hand, making the woman flinch before yanking her hand away. "What?"

"It's the safest place I could find," Haywood said as she exposed a handmade rope ladder. "You wanna stay down here? That's fine with me. Have fun with the compies and leeches."

Not bothering to listen to them, the red-haired woman easily clambered up the rope. She scaled it easily, making it clear this was part of her daily routine, and had been for a while.

"You heard the lady," Marshall said, nodding at Tanaka.

Stiffly returning the gesture, the Yakuza pulled himself up the mixture of vines, rope and fabric before disappearing into the plane. He didn't bother checking on the others. The man just entered the plane without hesitation.

"That boy's got an enormous set of balls," Dillahunt said before looking at Alvaradejo. "Up you go, Freddie."

A frantic shake of her head was her answer, and she stepped back, readying to flee into the jungle. Her reaction was understandable; the way they'd been delivered, the drop, then the pterodactyl attack would make anyone afraid of heights. But she was wasting time, and Marshall had questions for their new host.

"You'd rather take your chance out there instead of getting revenge?" he asked her, letting the implication do all the heavy lifting. If she was as ruthless as her file made her out to be, then that's all the motivation the woman would need.

Staring daggers at him, Alvaradejo muttered something in Spanish before scaling up the side of the tree. She moved easily, as if she'd been climbing all her life, and the moment she rolled over the precipice, both men heard a loud sigh of relief.

"What'd she say?"

Dillahunt shook his head before stepping forward. "Something about peeling layers of skin off Pendleton's cock before making them into a soup and feeding it to him," he said with a strange smile. "Fuck, I think I'm in love."

Marshall laughed as the man disappeared up the tree, then into the plane with no fuss, leaving him alone.

Turning away from the sanctuary, Marshall looked out at the jungle. His eyes scanned the trees, searching for any predator, and his mind conjured the image of the compies swarming Beaumont.

"Seamus! Get your ass up here," Dillahunt shouted, his voice filled with excitement and awe. "Seriously, get that Irish butt up here or you'll regret it for the rest of your life."

What the fuck? Marshall thought as he grabbed the rope ladder and hauled himself up towards the plane.

CHAPTER THIRTY-FIVE

Reaching the top, Marshall took a moment to regain his composure. It'd been forever since he'd done a rope climb, and he was glad his old CO and drill sergeant weren't there to see his terrible performance.

Rolling onto his front, he got to his feet and staggered across the threshold into the plane. The drastic change in lighting made him frown and blink while his eyes got used to the darker light.

He was standing in the rear of an old cargo plane. That much was obvious. The make of it, though, was something beyond his abilities. Rust and plant life covered most of the exterior and the interior was just as bad.

"What is it?" he asked, gasping for air as he searched for the others. Part of him feared it was a trap, but the tone of Dillahunt's voice made him think otherwise.

Haywood leaned against the side of the plane's hull. She looked relaxed and amused, watching the others. Not saying a word, she gestured with her hand and Marshall followed.

A large section of the plane's side was gone, torn away when it crashed years ago and the other three stood there, silently staring out at something.

"You'll love it," Haywood said as she stretched before standing. "I'll get food and water. Rest."

Nodding his gratitude, Marshall went over and stood next to Tanaka. He blinked, clearing his eyes and after a few seconds, he could see properly and gasped.

They were above the jungle canopy and he could see further than he had before. The jungle stretched on forever, but in the distance, he could see a mountain range slicing the clouds, towering over the rest of the island.

"It's fucking beautiful," Marshall said and his eyes focused on the group of majestic, long-necked dinosaurs grazing in front of them.

There were ten brachiosaurs, each of them doing their own thing and periodically they'd look at one another and bray. It reminded him of a cow's moo mixed with an elephant's trumpet, and Marshall smiled.

He felt at peace, and watching the gentle giants continue grazing and living their lives, reminded him of nature's true beauty.

It was an almost religious experience seeing the gentle giants going about their business. Especially after all they'd been through and the blood spilt in the name of sport. Part of him wanted to stay, enjoy the sight and exist. That was impossible, though, not until he rid the world of Charles Roy Pendleton.

"Now I know why you picked this place," he said, turning to face Haywood.

The woman was preparing a small gas-stove to cook a very basic meal, and instinctively, Marshall went over to her. Ignoring him, she stayed focused on making sure she had enough aluminium wrapped packets for the group

"That's one hell of a view," he said again, trying to make conversation. "Was that why you chose this place?"

Haywood laughed, then shook her head. "It is beautiful, but only if you keep your distance. The brachies and Apatosauruses are, in a way, more dangerous than the raptors or rex." She looked at the meagre set up then said, "Sorry. It's been forever since I've entertained anyone."

"How long have you been here?" Marshall asked, trying to get comfortable.

A high-pitched baby elephant-sounding bleating made him stop and, scrambling to his feet, he joined the others. Scanning the horizon, he saw a smaller brachiosaurus head break through the trees and look about, eagerly sharing its excitement.

"Anyone got a camera?" Dillahunt asked, wiping a tear from his eye. "Fuck woman, you chopping onions?"

Behind them, Haywood chuckled, then said, "Enjoy the show. They'll be there for another hour or so. Rest and regroup... that's how you say it, right? And I'll get the food ready."

Nodding, Marshall gave her a quick thumbs up before focusing on the pack of brachies slowly moving. It was the most glorious thing he'd seen and, in that moment, he felt closer to God than at any other point in his life.

If he or the others bothered to look up, though, they'd have noticed the drone hovering silently in the sky. Its camera was pointed at them, sending the details of their location and a live stream back to Pendleton.

CHAPTER THIRTY-SIX

Charles Roy Pendleton's hand squeezed his whisky glass tight. Staring at the image plastered on the big screen, he felt his grip tighten and the tumbler creak. If he kept the pressure up, the glass would shatter spectacularly and cut his hand badly.

"Inconceivable," he muttered, before turning away from the image of the plane and the survivors. To him, the situation had gone from exciting to acceptable to fucked in the space of hours. There was still time left, too much of it, and a sinking feeling filled his stomach.

Next to him, Carruthers cleared his throat softly. "Charles, it's not over until *you* say it's over," he said. "This is what you wanted."

He was right, and Pendleton knew it. The only problem was that the bounty hunter, Marshall, was rallying the others to follow him. If they found out the location of the compound, and a way past the dinosaurs, everything would be ruined.

Turning, Pendleton looked at the technician manning the drone's controls. "Where's that plane located?" he asked, stalking towards the nervous man.

Pendleton was barely aware of the other men in the room. None of them were as important as his prey. Seeing them safely above ground and out of reach of the more dangerous dinos irked.

If he knew where they were, then he'd be able to mount a frontal assault and take them out in one go.

"Sir?"

"The plane, where is it?" Pendleton said, doing his best to stay in control. The moment he lost his composure, the others would lose respect for him and then the hunts would be over. He'd have to go back to the real world, and that was unacceptable.

The young man stared at the tablet mounted on the drone controls and mumbled to himself as he found the tree's coordinates.

"The plane, boss! The plane!" Perkins bellowed, doing his best Tattoo impression from *Fantasy Island*. Around him, the others laughed and patted him on the back. It was clear they were drunk and enjoying themselves far too much.

Pendleton needed to fix that.

"Gentlemen," he said, turning away from the boffin. "As you can see, there's only four left. The most dangerous prey we've had. Unfortunately, though, it seems as if they've outsmarted the dinosaurs."

Pointing at the screen, the drone pulled away, giving them a better view of the area. "See, they're safely hidden from even the brachiosauruses! How can that be? Are we going to stand for it?"

"First you want a better class of plebes to hunt," Finaughty rumbled from behind his cigar "Then you won't let us go out to finish the job when we want to. But now, now that your money and reputation are on the line, you're going to send us out there. Bad form, Charles!"

Hearing the older man's words, the others mumbled their own grievances. Pendleton had to get them under control again, soon.

"Gentlemen," Pendleton said, holding up his hands defensively. "There's no need to cause a scene. We all agreed that this hunt was going to be different, and it has been. Certainly, the turn of events has been unexpected. But it's not over until the fat lady sings!"

As he spoke, Pendleton didn't notice the shocked looks slowly washing over the gathered men's faces.

"I promise you," he said, his voice rising in volume and fervour, "that by the end of the day, not the twenty-four hours, they shall be dead and you'll have your trophies. That's the Charles Roy Pendleton guarantee."

Expecting a stirring round of applause, Pendleton frowned at the silence. Looking at the frozen faces, a part of him wondered if the world had ended and this was his version of heaven? "Lads?"

"Charles," Carruthers said, tapping his employer on the shoulder. "You need to see this."

Turning to face his game warden, Pendleton saw the same stunned look on the man's face. Something was wrong.

"What is it?" Pendleton asked before turning to look at the screen. His eyes widened and his jaw dropped. He couldn't believe it. "No."

Haywood stood next to Marshall. It was clearly her. But she was supposed to be dead, eaten by the dinosaurs. At least that's what Carruthers told him. But there she was, standing proudly as if she owned the island. Master of her domain, so to speak, and he felt anger bubbling to the surface.

"She's the one who took them to the plane."

"Thank you for such an astute observation," Pendleton hissed, while fighting the urge to pummel his game warden. "She's supposed to be dead. What happened?"

Carruthers shook his head. Clearly, he had no answer and for a second Pendleton seriously considered throwing him and Finaughty to the dinosaurs. It would serve them right, but then again, he needed the able-bodied men to go out and take care of the prey.

That was it! A problem became the solution, and he smiled before squeezing Carruthers' shoulder.

"Head down to the armoury," Pendleton said softly. "Get the ATVs fuelled and loaded with extra cannisters. You're not coming back until the job's done."

With a stiff nod, Carruthers turned and quickly disappeared from the viewing room.

"Lads!" Pendleton said, standing in front of the screen again. "What an unexpected turn of events! When we thought all was lost, the gods of fortune smile down on us and deliver a bonus. Behold! Katherine Haywood. She of the flaming hair from four hunts ago. We all thought she was dead. At least, that's what Gerald Wiley told us all. Gerald?"

All eyes went to a middle-aged hunter sitting by himself. He looked out of place among the grandeur of the room and the expensive tailor-made clothes adorning the others. Wiley smiled at the group, saluted them with his cup before shrinking back into his chair.

"Fear not, Gerald. We all make mistakes," Pendleton said as his mind finalised the plan. "After all, to err is human, but to forgive is Pendleton."

The others chuckled nervously at the painful joke. It was perfunctory but part of the hunt's traditions, and one that Pendleton made use of to his full advantage.

"Now, this is the plan," he continued, bouncing slightly on his feet. "All standing bets are on. That hasn't changed. But the man who brings me the head of Katherine Haywood shall receive one hundred million dollars, and a place at the table."

That did it. As one, the gathered men stood cheering before filing out, leaving Pendleton alone.

Turning back to the screen, he watched the five people enter the plane. Now that he knew where they were, it would be simple to wipe them from the face of the earth. And if parting with a hundred million dollars was the price?

So be it.

CHAPTER THIRTY-SEVEN

"It's not much," Haywood said, serving the meagre meal, "but it's the best I can do."

Marshall nodded his thanks, taking the metal plate from the woman and the cup. She was right. The food didn't look anything special, but it would do the trick and fuel them. Holding the plastic spork, he poked and prodded the food, figuring out what was there.

"What is it?" Dillahunt asked as he held up a stringy piece of meat.

Looking at it, their host swallowed before saying, "Compy meat with some vegetables I found nearby. Don't worry, it's not poisonous."

Next to him, Alvaradejo shook her head and said, "It tastes like chicken. Just close your eyes and think it's fried." She took a big mouthful, chewed loudly, then swallowed. "At least it's not long pork."

Marshall smiled as he slowly ate. He felt the temptation to scoff down the meal, but his training told him not to. If they needed to move quickly, on a full stomach that was still digesting, they risked cramps.

"What's long pork?" Dillahunt asked, looking at the others. "Is it anything like barbecue?"

Tanaka shook his head. "Human meat."

The Southerner blinked, then laughed, spraying the Mexican in half-chewed food and saliva. She growled at him before shoving Dillahunt, sending him sprawling to the floor, still laughing.

"Cannibalism happens more often than you think," Haywood said. Her face was serious, and the others went quiet. "In any extreme survival situation, once food runs out, it doesn't take long for people to reach that level of desperation."

There was something in her voice that caught Marshall's attention and he said, "Is that what happened here? You and some others found this place and one thing led to another?"

"Nothing so dramatic," the woman said, shaking her head. "I found this place quickly and hid. Back then, there was food, drink and plenty of things to keep me occupied. But when those ran out, I ventured out to take care of myself. Survival of the fittest and all that."

"How long have you been here?"

Looking at the roof, Haywood was quiet and after a second, Marshall realised she was thinking. Finally, she nodded and looked at the man in the eyes. "Almost seven months."

Makes sense, Marshall thought as the others offered their condolences and words of comfort. It amazed him how quickly they were uniting, and strangely, taking care of each other. All of it was happening naturally, and he smiled. This was what they needed.

Haywood stayed quiet, almost embarrassed by the outpouring of affection, and she said, "You've all been trapped in a situation like this?"

"The Lacandon jungle is worse than this place," Alvaradejo said as she sipped from her cup. "Jaguars, lizards, snakes and tiny frogs that are so poisonous that there is no cure. But the people are monsters. Native tribes that rob and sell people to the cartels. Corrupt officials using the jungle for their own sadistic pleasures."

"Pendleton would fit in well with them," Marshall said softly. Before the Mexican could react, he turned to Haywood and said, "Seven months is a long time. You'd know the layout of the island, right?"

A small nod was the answer, and Marshall nodded, prompting her to speak.

"I was tired of teaching," Haywood said slowly. "But there wasn't enough money in my savings to do anything else. The job market," she said with a sad smile. "So, a friend of mine got me an interview at one of Pendleton's tech companies. During it, they offered me the deal of a lifetime. I was desperate."

She fought to control herself; tears formed in her eyes and her shoulders shook.

"Tell us about the island," Marshall said. He knew that if she focused her mind on something else, the fear and memories would subside. It was a tried-and-true tactic and the moment he said it, her eyes dried and she sniffed back the tears.

"I haven't been all over it. You keep to certain areas, otherwise the wildlife gets the better of you, and you've seen how that goes." Haywood chuckled, then shook her head, ridding her mind of the thoughts. "What do you want to know exactly?"

This was the question he was waiting for and hearing it, Marshall said, "Any buildings or structures that are of use to Pendleton? Is there a base of operations? What about defences and a way off the island?"

"Slow down there, Seamus," Dillahunt said, waving his hands as if he was distracting a bull at the rodeo. "The little lady here is overwhelmed, ain't you, love?" he asked, giving Alvaradejo a cheeky wink.

"No, I'm okay," Haywood said. She smiled at the group, then stood and went to the cockpit.

Looking about the plane, Alvaradejo laughed and pointed. Following her outstretched hand, the others saw a spray-painted symbol on the roof.

"This is the lost El Chapo plane!"

A cartel drug-running plane? Marshall thought as Haywood reappeared, clutching a piece of paper to her chest. He wanted to know more about the plane and its cargo, but getting a lay of the land and as much intel as possible was the priority.

"Is this helpful?" Haywood asked, handing Marshall a piece of paper.

His eyes scanned the page, and he felt himself nodding and smiling at the same time. It was roughly sketched using a mixture of pen and charcoal, but it was well drawn and clear enough to give him exactly what he needed.

"It's perfect," he said, showing the others the hand-drawn map of the island. A doodle of the plane with a red circle around it was their current location. Wiggly lines had to be the river and to the north, along the edge of the island, was a square box with Pendleton scrawled in it. A few other areas were marked, but that was all he needed to see.

"Let's get this shindig going," Dillahunt said, an enormous smile on his face, and Marshall felt the same. They could get to Pendleton and make him pay.

"Have you been there?" Alvaradejo asked, taking the page from Marshall. "What's the layout of the place?"

Haywood shook her head and held up her hands, silently apologising to them. "I don't know. I've only seen it from the outside and even then I couldn't linger. But they get deliveries that come in from behind."

"How?"

"Helicopters and boats, I think," Haywood answered, then sighed. Her shoulders slumped, and she shrunk as she said, "It won't matter, anyway. There are still the dinos."

CHAPTER THIRTY-EIGHT

As if on cue, the rumblings of the herbivores outside started again, adding the perfect exclamation point to the woman's statement. Under it, the six people could make out the chirping of smaller dinos and Marshall recognised the call of the compies.

"We can avoid them easily," Dillahunt said, holding up the map. "As long as we avoid the grassy knoll, nobody's going to lose their head."

He smiled at the others and, from their disapproving expressions, he went silent and handed the paper to Marshall. "I thought it made sense," the Southerner mumbled to nobody in particular.

He's got a point, Marshall thought as he studied the map. Without knowing what the scale was, it would be impossible to tell how far they'd have to travel. That meant the chances of getting attacked by the prehistoric monsters were too great a risk. Of course, if they stayed put, that brought a series of other troubles to deal with.

"I hate visits from Mister Cock-Up," he mumbled before rubbing his chin.

A grunt from Tanaka made the Irishman look up, and the tattooed killer said, "How many dinos are out there?"

It was an interesting question and the moment he asked it, Marshall knew it should've been his first one after meeting Haywood. One of the most important parts of planning a successful operation, whether with the SAS or as a bounty hunter, was knowing as much about the opposition's forces.

Without that knowledge, everything else was moot.

"I'm not sure," Haywood said, frowning in concentration. "I've only seen the compies, ankylosaurs, steggies, raptors, pachies and a few triceratopses. Of course, there are also the rexes, but they have their own territory."

"Not to mention the long necks," Dillahunt said, gesturing to the dinosaurs moving away from them. "It's a good menagerie, but doesn't help us."

Marshall shook his head. It did help, but he wasn't sure how exactly. That would require more time, and of course, detailed intel. All of it didn't matter, though, and he knew it. This was academic talk when the most important thing to focus on was the pheromones.

"Why is it the rex piss scares the other dinosaurs away?"

"Pheromones are chemicals that we produce, as do some other animals that can alter the way others behave and act. They affect brain chemistry in different ways and if potent enough, act like brainwashing drugs," Haywood said, and she seemed at ease. She was definitely a teacher. "Basically," she said, realising they weren't following the tech jargon, "the larger the predator, the more potent the pheromones are. It's a mixture of testosterone and their own scent. Same thing with big cats marking their territory "

Makes sense, Marshall thought as he nodded along with her explanation. Knowing how the stuff worked helped, but it still didn't give him enough to form a cohesive plan.

"So, if there was a bigger predator," Alvaradejo said slowly, "bigger than the T-Rex, its pheromones would scare it away?"

Haywood shook her head. "No, that would make it feel challenged, and it'd go looking for the interloper. In that case it'd have reason enough to fight and kill anything it perceived as a territorial invader."

"Then what stops it from killing all the long necks?" Dillahunt asked. He was leaning forward, completely focused on the woman, and his wide-eyed expression made him look like a child.

"Instinct," Haywood said, then frowned. "Actually, that makes sense. What they covered us in, the man-made pheromones make the dinosaurs, even the naturally docile ones, go crazy, right? It must be made up of certain parts of their natural aggressors and competitors. It's an engineering feat!"

Marshall wasn't sure what she was talking about, and looking at the others, it was clear they didn't know either. That fact alone made him feel better. Though it still didn't help them with how they were going to escape the dino infested island.

"Dumb it down for us?"

"Sorry," Haywood said, turning bright red. "So, what they did was take the pheromones from all the dinosaurs out there, picked certain aspects, the ones that would get the most violent reaction and put them all together. But they should've counteracted each other, unless they added a steroid to increase the potency."

It was clear Haywood was working on a different level to the others, and even though she was trying to make it simple for them to follow, she still failed.

"We'll take your word for it," Marshall said and waved his hand, signalling for her to stop. "Long story short," he said quickly, moving past the awkwardness. "is that if we find something bigger than the rex, we'll have a way to move about this place freely?"

Slowly, Haywood nodded, and Marshall smiled. It was better than nothing and meant they could begin properly planning their escape.

"Is there anything bigger than the rex?" Alvaradejo asked, beating Marshall to the punch.

"Not that I've seen. But it's not a problem," Haywood said, pointing to a jagged marking on the map. "That's their territory. All we need to do is avoid it at all costs. Otherwise, they'll see us as a threat, and meal."

"Of course," Marshall said. "Thanks, this is perfect," he said to Haywood before taking the map from her. Looking at the others, he tucked it into one of his vest's pouches.

"So, all we need to do is use pure T-Rex piss to make it there," Dillahunt said, then laughed. Next to him Tanaka joined in, then went silent the moment the Southerner added, "What could possibly go wrong?"

CHAPTER THIRTY-NINE

"A lot actually," Haywood said, holding Dillahunt's gaze. "For example, you could meet a herd of triceratops. They're not cute and cuddly like in *Jurassic Park*. No, these will use their horns to impale you before trampling you to death."

Her words conjured a vivid image, and Marshall shivered at the picture. "Okay, you made your point, we'll be—"

"Then there are the raptors," she continued, talking over Marshall. "You saw what they did to the rest of your group. If you go off course and stumble into one of their nests, it won't matter what you are. They'll hunt you down and vivisect you before having lunch."

"Are there Dilophosauruses?" Tanaka asked. His voice was soft as he spoke, almost like he was afraid to say it out loud.

Haywood looked at him, then nodded. "There are at least two that I've seen. You've seen the first *Jurassic Park* movie?" she asked and when the man nodded, she continued. "The movie got it wrong. They don't spit a paralytic agent. It's a highly concentrated form of stomach acid, I think. You don't want to get in their way. Trust me," she said and showed them puckered scars on her forearm.

"Is that enough, or should I go on?" Haywood said, turning her attention back to Dillahunt.

Slowly, he shook his head and said, "No, ma'am."

"Right," Marshall said, slapping his thighs to get everyone's attention, "now that we've been vividly informed as to the dangers out there, we need to figure out how we're going to get to the compound and then off the island. Any suggestions?"

The silence that greeted him was as deafening as the roars of the charging Ankylosaurus and Stegosaurus. It wasn't what Marshall expected, and he looked at the individual faces of the men and women. Each of them wore a similar expression of uncertainty. None wanted to be the first to speak, which was something Marshall was used to.

"It's simple," he said, unfolding the piece of paper and laying it flat on the palm of his hand. "We'll do the same thing Haywood did to the raptors."

Haywood shook her head. "I'm out of smoke bombs," she said before looking out at the jungle.

"Not a problem," Marshall said, and he meant it. "All we need is the rex piss. That'll drive off the dinos and give us the cover we need to reach the compound. Once inside, we find Pendleton, then get the fuck out before anyone's the wiser."

It was a good plan, as far as he was concerned. Naturally, it would require some finessing.

The others nodded as they stared at the map, each of them working through different scenarios and permutations of the idea. Marshall studied their faces. If any had a problem, or a better idea, it'd show before they spoke.

"It's simple," Alvaradejo said with a curt nod of her head. "But we're going to need weapons, just in case any of the dinos get too bold."

Haywood stood. "I've got that sorted."

All eyes stayed on her as she walked over to a wooden crate. Lifting a latch, the woman grunted as she opened the lid and let it flop backwards. A loud slap filled the confined space, and the group winced.

Marshall was the first to reach it and, peering inside, he grinned like it was Christmas. The crate held a collection of ammo boxes, magazines, grenades, and weapons. He spotted Glocks, Desert Eagles and Tokarev pistols, another MP5 sub-machine gun, FN-Scar L and HK416 rifles and what looked like a Mossberg shotgun.

"That'll do nicely," he said before pulling out a handful of magazines. His MP5 was still attached to the vest, and quickly he switched it for the HK416. He slid a Tokarev TT-33 pistol into a side holster.

Now Marshall felt able to defend himself.

"What about getting in?" Tanaka asked as he picked up two large machetes. He spun them, feeling the weight and balance, and smiled.

"It's fortified," Haywood said, shaking her head. "A large fence, heavy duty gate and guard towers. Plus, I once saw turrets that were unmanned. You'd need a tank or airstrike to get through it."

"Or a distraction," Marshall mumbled as he watched the others load up. It was curious, and in a way fascinating, for him to watch Dillahunt and Alvaradejo take certain weapons. The Mexican loaded herself up with grenades, the Mossberg and a couple of the SIG-Sauer P239 pistols. As for Dillahunt, he went for a HK P30 handgun and then took an FN SCAR-L rifle.

Turning away from them, Marshall wished the Russian was still alive. He'd make the perfect distraction and would've bought them enough time to get through the perimeter defences.

Doesn't matter, he thought, folding the paper up again. *He's dead. Deal with it and figure out something else.*

"Then we need to figure out a way to get through the gates and into the compound." Dillahunt's voice made Marshall turn, and the Southerner smiled at him.

"You got any ideas, bud?"

The smile disappeared, and Dillahunt nodded. "You don't end up working for the Dixie Mafia without learning a thing or two about dealing with poachers or farmers."

"What the fuck does that mean?" Alvaradejo asked, her head tilted to the side like a confused dog. "I've never heard of the Dixie Mafia, let alone a gringo having to deal with farmers."

For a split second, Marshall saw pain cross Dillahunt's face, then vanish as he laughed and smiled again. "Little lady," he said, exaggerating his drawl. "I bet there's a bunch of stuff you ain't never heard of. But have a little faith. Ol' Walt's got you sorted."

"Get on with it," Marshall said, shaking his head. They were running out of time, and a looming feeling of dread formed in the pit of his stomach.

"Sorry, hoss," the other man said, instantly dropping the over-the-top southern accent. "The best way to get through any structure, especially fences, is to use explosives. Now, if you don't have any, what's the next best thing?"

He looked eagerly at the others, who stared back at him blankly. A frown creased Dillahunt's brow, and he finally said, "Animals! What we need to do is get a stampede going."

CHAPTER FORTY

"Let me see if I understand," Marshall said the moment his voice worked again. "You're saying that we need to rustle up some dinosaurs, point them in the right direction, and what? Slap them on the ass and hope they run?"

"It's not as simple or cartoony as you put it," Dillahunt said, standing. He arched his back, stretching, then sighed in relief. "But yeah. That's about right. Nobody's going to fuck with a couple tonnes of dinosaur barrelling down on them."

It was so simple, yet crazy as fuck, that Marshall wasn't sure it'd work. On some level, though, he knew Dillahunt was on the right track. If there were turrets, then a dinosaur, especially multiple ones, could take care of them easily.

"For a gringo, you're one crazy motherfucker," Alvaradejo said, shaking her head. "How are you planning on getting them in place, or even agitated enough to run?"

Haywood added her own opinion before Dillahunt could answer. "Not to mention that to get close enough, you'd have to make sure the dinos couldn't smell you. But even then, it'd be impossible to know if they'd go in the right direction. Too many variables."

It was good they were punching holes in the plan. It made the originator of the idea work to find answers while also letting the others in the group have their say. Marshall did this with his squad and it always ended with a better plan. One that had a higher rate of success.

"And once they broke through," Alvaradejo was saying, "how do you make sure they don't destroy buildings? I have a plan for *Señor* Pendleton."

Marshall's eyes went to Dillahunt, and he felt sorry for the man. What was supposed to be a genius plan was being ripped to shreds one piece at a time. But they didn't have another plan, which meant they had to make this one work.

And that, as far as Marshall was concerned, was a tall order.

"It'll work." Tanaka's voice silenced the women instantly. He sat crossed-leg with the machetes resting across his knees. "It'll work," he repeated and nodded at Dillahunt. "A stampede is more dangerous than any bomb or tank. All forces of nature are like that. Respect the animals, even extinct ones, and they will deliver."

"That's what I was saying," Dillahunt said, beaming as he moved to be closer to the Yakuza. "I knew there was a reason I liked you, Joey!"

Ignoring the smiling man, Tanaka continued talking. "The Tyrannosaurus Rex urine will do the trick. It'll scare the dinosaurs we need, and by following, we can steer them."

"What dinosaurs?" Marshall asked. He liked the idea more and more, but needed all the details.

"The ankylosaurs, steggies, triceratops and the long necks would work perfectly," Haywood said. Her eyes were bright with ideas and a grin threatened to slice her face in half. "They're the only ones on the island that would be threatened enough by the rex to bolt. Of course, they're not the fastest, though."

Nodding along with her train of thought, Marshall said, "But that won't matter. Get them running early enough and their bulk will do all the work."

The more they talked, Marshall became certain that this was the way to go. It didn't matter what Pendleton's defences were, or if the turrets used heavy ordinances. The dinosaurs were the best option for them and even if some were killed, it wouldn't matter.

It was perfect in every way.

"What about the raptors and compies?" Alvaradejo asked, staring out at the jungle. Her eyes were focused on the middle distance. "Should we be worried about them?"

"Not in the slightest. The raptors would never get into a fight with a rex. Unless, once again, we trampled their nests. Even then, the tanks would cover us," Haywood said, before pursing her lips.

Marshall saw the look and said, "What is it?"

"The only problem is if we get trampled. It's going to be hard judging speed and keeping all of them moving at the same pace."

"Not a problem, darling," Dillahunt said, a wicked smile on his lips. "Every now and then, we just give them a nip on the rear. That'll keep 'em moving."

Marshall smiled as he worked through the plan in his mind. Using the T-Rex piss, they'd have to round up the dinosaurs, which would be done in smaller groups and then brought together. After that, all that needed to be done was steer them straight at Pendleton. It was a simple plan, with barely any moving parts, but he felt as if he was missing something important.

"Problem?" Tanaka said, his voice shattering Marshall's thoughts. "Is there a problem with the plan?"

Before he could look at Haywood, the woman said, "Theoretically it'll work. But apart from the defences and even the logistics of dino wrangling, there's a problem."

Fucking knew it, Marshall thought, gesturing for her to continue speaking.

"I'm out of rex piss. I used the last of my supplies saving your asses."

"Then we go out and get some more," Dillahunt said, getting to his feet. He stretched, rolling his neck and shoulders before picking up his rifle. "It must be easy to get pissed on by a rex, right? Just stand under it and wait."

Once again, Marshall was amazed by the man's simplistic way of looking at the world. It did make sense though. How else did one collect dinosaur urine?

"How did you get it in the first place?" he asked, turning to Haywood.

The woman turned bright red and looked away before saying, "Wasn't easy."

Fuck, Marshall thought as he slumped into a mould-covered decrepit chair. It groaned under his weight and he waited for it to collapse. When it didn't, he sighed and looked at the others; each of them had the same disappointed look on their faces and he knew there wasn't another way to get to Pendleton.

Not unless we were to draw him out and use the element of surprise. It was an interesting idea, but there was no way of knowing exactly how many men Pendleton had with him. Or what weapons they carried.

Without that knowledge, they were shit out of luck.

"It's possible that it *could* work," Haywood said. She stood, looking out at the jungle. The fingers on her left hand twitched and wriggled like she was performing calculations.

"What's possible?" Marshall asked, leaning forward. His back ached, and he realised that his body was stiff. Even though they weren't running for their lives, he hadn't rested yet. And from the way the woman mumbled to herself, it was clear he wouldn't for a while longer.

Haywood turned to face the others, a wild look in her eyes, and she grinned. "It'll work," she said with a firm nod. Ignoring the questioning looks from the four, she went to the rear of the plane and unrolled the ladder.

"Let's go," she said, waiting for them to follow her orders. "Chop chop!"

CHAPTER FORTY-ONE

The sun was high in the sky, almost past the noon mark, and Marshall rolled his arms. There was plenty of time before dusk and he suspected Haywood didn't want to be out in the open at night.

Ahead of him, the red-haired woman led them once more. Moving with a purpose, Haywood ignored everything except the path they needed to take. She leapt and bounded over fallen trees and broken stumps.

It was impressive watching her move, and there was a nervous energy about the way she sped through the jungle. Marshall could feel it radiating from her, and he knew it was affecting the others.

Looking back, he said, "How're we doing? Feeling good about the plan?"

"Sure thing, Seamus," Dillahunt said, ducking under a vine. He came up and cursed, swatting a thin branch covered in leaves from his face. "Fucking cunt fucker! I can't wait to get back home and drink myself into a stupor."

"One drink and you're done?" Alvaradejo said, then laughed. A little behind her, bringing up the rear, Tanaka chuckled, then looked about, making sure they were safe.

Dillahunt gasped, then said, "How dare you impugn my ability to drink! I'm shocked you'd say such a thing. Absolutely shocked." His face broke into a large grin. "Tell you what, I bet I can drink you under the table faster than you can me."

"*Guapo*," Alvaradejo said, looking him up and down, "you couldn't handle this."

Before their flirting could continue, Marshall cleared his throat. "You two finished? Or should we wait for the inevitable coitus and devouring of Walt's head?"

Tanaka exploded into laughter. His body trembled as he snorted, fighting to control himself. As he laughed, Marshall brought up the HK416 and flicked the safety off. His shoulders tensed and he noticed both Alvaradejo and Dillahunt ready themselves.

"Keep it the fuck down!" Haywood hissed. "We're not in Kansas anymore and sounds like that," she said, pointing at Tanaka, "are the perfect way of getting us all eaten!"

Not bothering to wait for an answer, she turned and started jogging. It was clear she didn't care if they caught up to her, and Marshall felt like an idiot for letting the situation get out of control.

"Forgive me," Tanaka said solemnly, before bowing. "I've dishonoured us all with my carelessness. Accept my apology, please."

Shaking his head, Marshall waved the others to go ahead and said to the Yakuza, "It's okay, Joe. Sometimes we need a good laugh to relieve the tension. Let's just keep it to a chuckle from now on, okay?"

"Yes," Tanaka said before following the others.

Watching the three catch up to their guide, Marshall ran through the plan once more. Wherever Haywood was leading them to, obviously it had something useful and a part of him hoped it wasn't a piss bath.

Not the worst thing you've done, he thought, then shuddered. The sense memory of the biting cold in Siberia came to him and he hurried after them, focusing his mind on the present and immediate future.

The hardest part of the plan, as far as he was concerned, was going to be rounding up the dinosaurs. It was clear he'd have to split them up into teams and assign a meeting place, but there were too many variables to consider. If any of them went the wrong way, or got caught in the stampede, it would be lights out and game over.

"Not on my watch," Marshall mumbled. It didn't matter what happened, he'd figure out a way to get everyone, including Haywood, off the island.

Reaching the others, he slowed his pace and fell into rhythm with them. Everyone was silent, Haywood's scolding still fresh, and he realised they didn't want to anger her even more.

"How do we get the dinos in place?" Marshall asked Dillahunt. He spoke loudly enough for the others to hear, but not too loud that he'd attract any monsters.

"No way in hell I'm doing that on my own. But I know you'll figure it out, Seamus. That's what you're good at," the other man said with a big grin. He winked at Marshall before spinning out of Haywood's way.

The woman stood still, one hand raised in a fist. It was the internationally recognised signal to stop, and the others halted. Slowly, she lowered the limb and brought a finger to her lips, shushing them.

"What is it?" Marshall asked, standing next to her.

Silently, Haywood pointed to the jungle in front of them. Even though they were following a trail, the foliage made it hard to see more than a few metres ahead of them and Marshall realised it was perfect for an ambush.

"Weapons ready," he said. His rifle snapped up, and he lowered himself into a firing stance.

Behind him, he heard the tingling of metal as the others readied themselves for a fight. Part of him hoped it was Pendleton's men. He was tired of the dinosaurs.

His luck wasn't that good, though.

He opened his mouth to ask Haywood what was going on, when a high-pitched squeak stopped him.

The sound continued, and it reminded him of a dolphin's call. A series of whistles, clicks and squeaks that sounded like talking wafted through the jungle.

Next to him, he felt Haywood stiffen.

The woman trembled slightly; she glanced behind her, staring at the other four. "Dilophosaurs. Run."

CHAPTER FORTY-TWO

Crashing through the jungle, Marshall had no idea where they were going. All he knew was that the Dilophosaur's call followed them. It wasn't like anything he'd heard before; it sounded friendly, like a family pet waiting for its master.

"It sounds cute," Haywood said, gasping for air, "but trust me, that thing will kill you first chance it gets."

He believed her and, looking behind him, said, "Walter, cover the rear. Frederica, stay in the middle." He watched as Dillahunt slowed until Tanaka passed him. The Yakuza held both machetes at the ready and waited for his orders.

"Cover our sides," Marshall ordered. Even though there was only the single dinosaur tracking them, and it was definitely doing that, there was always the chance the compies would appear and swarm them.

"Safeties off," he hissed to the Mexican, who nodded, then passed the order along to Dillahunt.

"Oh, was I supposed to wait for that order?" the other man said, chuckling. "What the fuck? Now there's two of them?"

Another slightly deeper version of the dino's call started, this time though, it sounded sinister, as if the Dilophosaurus was a fighter and ready to attack at a moment's notice. If that was the case, Marshall was ready to let it know who was boss.

"This way," Haywood said, turning and putting the sounds behind them. She increased her speed until they were galloping through the jungle.

This is crazy, Marshall thought, pushing himself to keep up with the woman. Being trapped on an island with only a finite amount of territory to explore, most of it being jungle, for six months made her a natural at navigating it. For him and the others? It was hard work and he could feel sweat rolling down his spine.

Haywood slowed and looked about frantically. Dropping to a knee, she inspected the ground, then looked at a tree trunk. A second later, she nodded, then took off in the opposite direction.

Passing it, Marshall saw a strange symbol carved into the bark. *Smart*, he thought, leaving markers to guide her if she was lost or in a panic. It would be stupid to not follow her and as his legs moved, he heard a third trilling fill the air.

There were now three of the dinosaurs after them, and Marshall suspected they knew what they were doing. Was it possible the Dilophosauruses were herding them towards a kill box?

"Hey," he said to the woman leading them. "Do these things usually hunt in packs?"

A quick shake of the head was Haywood's answer. Marshall wasn't sure if that was a no to his question or if she was saying she didn't know in general. Either way, he didn't feel confident that they weren't being led by the nose.

A fourth Dilophosaurus chirped to their left and Haywood yelped in fright.

Not thinking, Marshall squeezed the trigger and felt his rifle kick. The roar of the short burst mixed with the sounds of leaves being shredded filled the air, and his nose caught the pungent stench of burnt gunpowder.

"Everything okay?"

Holding up a thumb, Marshall turned to Haywood and said, "Keep moving. You know this place better than us. Don't stop until we get to wherever the fuck you're taking us."

The woman blinked, then nodded as her eyes became thin slits of determination. This was what Marshall was best at, rallying the troops to get the results he needed. Which in this case was making sure Haywood kept moving.

Hope we get there soon, he thought, ducking under another branch. His breathing was ragged and his torso ached. If he kept going, Marshall was positive he'd puke and the stench of undigested food would attract more than the dinos.

"Shit!" Haywood said, sliding to a halt. She held both arms out, creating a barrier, and Marshall crashed into her.

"What the fuck, woman?" Marshall said before going silent. Behind him, he felt the others slow, then stop. "Nobody move a muscle."

Ahead of them were four dinosaurs. They were shorter than the raptors, but looked equally dangerous. Like the fast hunters, these dinosaurs stood on two legs, with the front ones curled under the chest, like arms. A large crest ran along their snouts, giving them an alien appearance and as they looked at the five people, they trilled and made the dolphin-like sounds.

"That's a Karensaurus?" Dillahunt asked, then looked at the incredulous looks on the others' faces. "What? You said they spit, right? My ex, Karen, spat a fuckton, so, Karensaurus."

"Shut the fuck up," Marshall hissed as he slowly raised his gun. If he could scare them off with a single shot, life would be easier, but as he readied to fire, he saw that one of the Dilophosaurs had fresh scratches gouged into its neck.

He must've wounded it earlier.

Fuck, he thought as the dinos sniffed the air. Any second now they'd smell the pheromones and attack. Which meant he, the Mexican and Dillahunt, needed to be ready for anything. If they were spitters, like Haywood said, then they'd have to get in close enough.

That was their only advantage over the dinos.

The bleeding Dilophosaurus took a step forward and shrieked as a large frill opened around its neck. Gone was the cute dolphin sound. Now it was a hissing mixed with a raspy howl, and Marshall wanted to flee.

"Fuck this," he muttered and lifted the rifle. At the same time, he saw Tanaka step in front of them, raising his blades. "Get the fuck back!"

"No," Joe Tanaka said with a shake of his head. "I did this. My laugh brought them to us, and it must be me who sends them to hell. Not you."

Turning away from them, Marshall watched the Yakuza utter a war cry as he ran towards the startled group of dinosaurs. His machetes spun, and the sunlight bounced off them creating a beautiful, hazy effect.

"What do we do?" Dillahunt asked, as the other three Dilophosaurs snarled, then roared as their frills snapped open.

CHAPTER FORTY-THREE

Tanaka closed the distance between himself and the four dinosaurs. His eyes darted between each of them as he studied their movements. Most people believe that the best way to fight someone is by watching their face. This is far from the truth, and the Yakuza knew this. It was the first thing he was taught the day he approached Kaoru Orochi, and demanded to be part of the Shibukawa Yakuza clan.

After years of training, and countless trips to the hospital, Tanaka knew that the only way to predict what an opponent would do was to focus on their chest. Their breathing gave everything away. This was what he did as he ran towards the Dilophosaurs.

Behind him, he could feel the others' presence and silently begged them to move. If he fell, which was a possibility, then the others would be easy prey. This, he did not want to haunt his spirit in the next world.

The wounded dinosaur's head reared back, and its neck swelled Its hissing became a gurgling sound and the animal's neck pulsed before it spat.

Seeing the movement, Tanaka side-stepped the attack and wrinkled his nose as the fetid stench of bile and stomach acid passed him. Dropping into a slide, he opened his arms wide and sliced at the air, aiming for the dinos' legs.

Startled yelps came from the Dilophosaurs, and they bounced away. The movement reminded him of kangaroos, and another of the dinos hurled acid at him.

Pushing off the ground, he flipped, then landed on the toes of his right foot. At the same time, he swung the machetes, cutting an X pattern in the air. He felt some resistance, followed by something warm and wet splattering his arms.

A pain-filled wail came from one of the dinosaurs and looking, Tanaka saw its left arm hanging limply by a string of flesh.

Pushing his advantage, the Yakuza soldier stabbed both blades at the Dilophosaurus while kicking back with his leg. He needed to keep in his head that these were wild animals, not trained fighters like the men back in Osaka.

He felt the blades tremble as they slid into the dinosaur's chest, puncturing its lungs, filling them with blood.

It gurgled, then spat. All that came out was blood, and the Dilophosaurus wobbled before slumping to the ground. A spasm wracked its body before the dinosaur uttered a death rattle and went still.

With a grunt, Tanaka yanked his knives from the dead animal, then a grin threatened to slice his face in half as he flung the blood off them. He finished the move, dropping into a crouch, ready to receive the next attack.

In front of him was the wounded dinosaur. Its eyes were thin slits, and it hissed at him, then quickly flicked its head to the left and right. The man knew that on either side of him were the other dinos and he angled his blades so they were pointed at them.

"*My ancestors will be proud,*" he said softly in Japanese before kicking dirt, bark and dried leaves at the lead dinosaur.

The animal screeched and battered the detritus from its face.

Ignoring it, Tanaka performed a roundhouse kick at the dinosaur on his right and felt the blow connect. Quickly, he landed another, then darted away.

A hacking sound came from his left and, reacting faster than he thought was possible, he threw one of the machetes at the dinosaur.

He heard a dull thud followed by a sickening wet crunch. Risking a look, Tanaka saw the dinosaur lying on the ground, the machete buried in its head, lodged between its crest.

A sizzling filled the air, and he cried out as his right arm exploded with pain. It felt on fire and looking, he saw a black liquid covering his forearm. It bubbled and sizzled, and the stench of burning bacon filled his nostrils.

Gritting his teeth, Tanaka took the knife in his left hand and looked at the Dilophosaurus.

The dinosaur glared at him, its frill fully extended. It snarled at him before lowering itself for another attack.

Joe Tanaka screamed at the dinosaur, his voice cracking from the rage and pain he felt, and the animal backed away and looked at the other one. That was his opening, and the man flung his dead arm at the animal.

Blood splattered its snout, and the Dilophosaurus grunted, lowering its frill. It never saw the cold blue steel of the machete flash, severing its jugular.

A fountain of blood erupted from the wound, and with a gurgling cry, the dinosaur collapsed. Dead before it hit the ground.

Standing over it, Tanaka's blood-covered visage made him look like a demon and his eyes found the others. They were moving away from him, doing as he bid. Except for Marshall. The man stood there, watching him

132

fight. Honouring him, one warrior to another.

Tanaka heard a snarl, followed by the wet hacking sound. He was too late in turning and his left leg burned before he collapsed.

"Joe!" he heard Marshall shout, but there was nothing to be done. This was his destiny. The Yakuza soldier was ready for it, and nodded at the Irishman to go.

Turning away from the sight of the man fleeing into the jungle, Joe Tanaka of the Shibukawa clan stared up into the yellow eyes of the final Dilophosaurus. The scratches along its neck were already congealing with blood and a slither of drool mixed with acid ran from its lower jaw.

Gathering up all of his remaining strength, Tanaka bellowed at the animal as it launched itself at him.

The last thing he felt, as the pointed teeth punctured his flesh, severing the veins in his neck, was a sense of release and honour. Tanaka had made his ancestors proud

CHAPTER FORTY-FOUR

"Well, that's a big pile of shit," Dillahunt said, wrinkling his nose at the stench of faeces wafting through the area. "Are we sure this is the only way?"

Marshall shook his head. Of course, it would be the Southerner who cracked a joke. Every squad had a member like that. The one person who couldn't help themselves and had that natural inclination to make others laugh.

In front of them, he saw the collection of shit stacks. There were five of them, each over two metres tall. Swarms of flies covered the tops of the piles, feasting on the bounty and laying maggots. It was disgusting, knowing what they were about to do, but for Marshall it was completely necessary.

"The sooner you get this over with, the sooner you can wash off," Haywood said, standing to the side. She smiled at the three as they passed her, and Marshall knew she was enjoying herself.

"You're not going to join?"

The redhead shook her head before looking around. "Someone's got to make sure nothing with teeth shows up to cause problems."

Hearing this, both Alvaradejo and Dillahunt spun to stare at the woman. Their weapons were ready to fire. Their eyes were wild with tension and adrenaline. Marshall shook his head before signalling for them to relax.

"You said nothing would come here!" Dillahunt said, as he turned to face a pile of excrement. He looked it up and down, then shuddered. "Maybe we should just fight our way through their defences."

Next to him, the Mexican snorted, then placed her weapons and spare ammunition on the ground. Standing, she stretched before looking at the Southerner. "Either grow some balls, *güero*, and dive in, or swallow the barrel of your rifle. It's that simple."

Before Dillahunt could react, Alvaradejo threw herself into the steaming pile of shit. A wet squish sounded, and she gagged. Taking a deep breath, the dark-haired woman rolled and gathered up more of the poo, rubbing it over her.

"That's an interesting lady," Haywood said softly. "Makes you wonder about her life."

Marshall watched Dillahunt slowly drop his own weapons, then empty his pockets before slowly covering himself in T-Rex crap. He scooped it up and began rubbing it onto his legs, taking his time and making sure every inch of him was covered.

"Just fucking dive in, buddy!" Marshall said. He chuckled at the sight of Dillahunt wobbling precariously on one leg, a clump of dark brown poo in his hands.

Turning away from the comical sight, Marshall looked at Haywood. "We can get you off the island and back home. Wherever that is."

Shaking her head, Haywood looked away, focusing her gaze on a large three-toed footprint, then sighed. "It's a kind offer, but I'm positive they declared me dead and have moved on."

It would be better to take his time, Marshall reasoned, so he slowly began disarming himself. There was something going on with the woman in front of him and he needed to know what it was. If it was a liability, then he had to know now.

"What is it?" he asked, forcing himself to stay focused on the woman and the insane plan they had. "I'd have thought you'd be racing to get out of this hell?"

"It doesn't matter," Haywood said after an uncomfortable second. Her eyes were red, brimming with tears and her chin trembled. Whatever was going on, it was serious, and Marshall had a feeling what it might be about.

Unclipping his rifle, Marshall handed it to the woman and said, "You were married? Family?"

Haywood opened her mouth, but her voice caught in her throat so instead, she nodded and gripped the rifle's stock.

"It was just us three. Ronald, Casey and myself. The three musketeers, she called us," Haywood said softly. To Marshall it sounded as if she was remembering a sweet dream, but was having problems with specific details. He'd seen this before and knew the best thing to do was let her go at her own pace.

"She's amazing. My Casey. Such a sweetheart with the biggest imagination you could find. Dinosaurs, that's what she was focused on. Couldn't get enough of them and, well, she'd love this place."

"Except for the fact they'd want to eat her."

A small laugh came from Haywood. "She'd never make it. The last time I saw her, she was going in for dialysis. I was supposed to pick her up, but I got the offer for this and went for it."

"She's sick?"

"Yes," Haywood's voice was emotionless, but her eyes were alight with fury and a profound sadness. "That's the reason I did this. A

135

guarantee she'd have the best medical care we could find. My Casey would have a life."

Placing a hand on her knee, Marshall smiled at her. "We'll get you back to her. The two musketeers doesn't have the right ring to it."

Ignoring her protests, Sean Marshall turned, allowing the vest to slide off his shoulders and thud to the ground. His eyes were on a fresh steaming pile of shit and steeling himself for the disgusting task ahead, he spun and fell backwards into it.

Feeling the excrement embrace him, he scooped up handfuls of the foul-smelling stuff and began rubbing it onto his chest. Once they finished here, all they'd need to do was round up the dinos.

Easy, Marshall thought.

CHAPTER FORTY-FIVE

The cigar bounced as Charles Roy Pendleton gnawed on it. The tobacco crunched from the force of his jaws and he tasted the dried leaves. A smile crept along his mouth as he puffed on the smoke, enjoying the sensations and flavours of Nicaragua's finest export.

Picking up his glass, the moustached man sipped the amber liquid and winced from the burn. Once the others had left the armoury, he'd broken out the good stuff and was enjoying a quiet moment of peace before the final slaughter.

It has to be a slaughter, he thought, walking towards the theatre room. If any of the prey survived, he'd be ruined. If most of the hunters were wiped off the face of the planet then he would start again rebuilding the hunts into something befitting the 21st century.

His footsteps sounded like the clip-clop of a horse's hooves and he smiled. Once he was finished with this, he'd go back to the ranch in Montana, and his horses.

Yes, he thought as he saw the blue glow of the large screen growing in size. *That's what I'll do. Ride and start working on the modern version of the hunt.*

Taking the cigar out of his mouth, Pendleton said, "Bring up the drones. We need a fix on their location. Now. Or would you rather I send you out to be tonight's entertainment?" His eyes bore into the back of the boffin's head, forcing the man to turn and stare at him.

"Yes, Mister Pendleton. I'm working on it right now, sir." The boffin's voice cracked as his hand pressed a series of buttons on a touch-screen panel and the screen flickered, shuffling through different images. Each was from a different drone, and they all showed the same thing; the island, but no humans.

Pendleton frowned. This wasn't right. "What about the scanners?"

Another flurry of movement from the young man and the screen went dark for a second. When it became bright again, it showed a series of different graphs and charts.

"What's that supposed to mean?"

Swallowing, the technician pointed to the far-left collection of data. "That's the heat charts. They're in normal parameters for this time of year. Whenever the hunt's on, we take the core body temperature of us and them and create a formula that makes sure we get viable data," he said before tapping a button. "This is the last hunt's reports. As you can see, the readings were off the roof."

"Of course," Pendleton rumbled before placing the cigar back in his mouth. "How did we lose them? We knew where they were. What the hell happened?"

It was a damn good question and one that any sane person would ask. Placing a hand on the boffin's shoulder, Pendleton squeezed as he asked, "What the hell happened?"

"Sir," the technician said before yelping from the pain as Pendleton's fingers curled around his collarbone. "It's not my fault. The drone we had locked onto them needed to recharge its battery. Normally when that happens, it sends a signal out and another takes its place."

"So?"

"Well, either they knew it was there and waited for an opportunity to give us the slip. Or—"

"Or they got lucky," Pendleton said, finishing the man's sentence. Grunting in frustration, he released the boffin before pinching the bridge of his nose. It wasn't going according to his plan and a part of him wished he had listened to Carruthers and brought in mercenaries.

At least then he'd have a guaranteed back-up.

"Find Carruthers and the rest of those useless tits," Pendleton barked as he finished his drink. Staring at the screens, his eyes focused on the flashing images, hoping he'd catch a break and finally get some good news.

He could keep up the charade of being in control for only so much longer.

"Sir," the boffin said as he brought up security camera footage. There they were, Carruthers and a line-up of armed men sitting on top of ATVs like they were in the cavalry.

"Carruthers," he said into the microphone. "How are we looking?"

Watching the game warden fumble with his own equipment, Pendleton said to the technician, "Get a drone down there. I want to see everything."

He saw the young man's fingers dance across the controls and the image switched to that of the hi-res crystal-clear view of an aerial shot. It descended towards the front of the compound, along the perimeter, giving him the perfect view of the group and his defences.

"Sir, no sign of them yet," Carruthers said. "We've been out here a good ten minutes now, and it's a ghost town." He looked up at the drone and shrugged.

Pendleton shook his head then said to the boffin, "How many drones are currently active?"

"About twenty, sir. With a contingency of another fifteen, should we need them." The young man rubbed his tired eyes, then said, "What are you thinking?"

It was clear to Pendleton now. These weren't only men with training, each of them had particular skill-sets. Ones that made them dangerous for men like Pendleton and his ilk. Why else would the cartel use a woman like Frederica Alvaradejo?

"We need to flush them out," Pendleton said softly before looking at the technician. "I want every single one of them out there. Have them buzzing the jungle, the plains, the mountain and the river. Follow the coastlines too. I want them found."

Turning to the microphone again, he said, "Have you sent out any recon teams?"

"No, Charles. I haven't done that because I'm an idiot who doesn't know his elbow from his arsehole."

"Don't get smart with me," Pendleton said, his voice a low growl. "Have you heard from them?"

Watching the screen, he saw Carruthers shake his head. This was wrong on so many levels. It was impossible for anyone to simply disappear on his island. He'd given themselves all the advantages modern technology allowed and yet, four people were able to stay off the radar and his drones' scanners.

"Inconceivable," Pendleton muttered again before turning away from the tech boffin and screens. If his father and grandfather could see him now, they'd be disappointed, and he knew who was to blame.

A beeping started, sounding like a clock's alarm. It grew in volume with each second, becoming shriller.

Spinning to tell the boffin to shut it down, Pendleton saw the control panel light up and all he could say was, "What's that?"

CHAPTER FORTY-SIX

"What's going on?" Pendleton repeated as another alarm began to blare. One after another, the control panel flashed, looking like a DJ's set-up and the young man in front of it scrambled to get everything under control.

Using his sleeve to wipe sweat from his face, the boffin looked at the screen, tapped the controls and brought up a graph. It fluctuated erratically but spiked into the reds.

"It's the seismic alarm," he finally said, voice trembling. "See," he said before showing a radial graph that pulsed and spasmed.

"Earthquake?"

The man shook his head and cycled through the different scanners and systems in place across the island. It was one of the few things that Pendleton made sure of; there was no way he'd be caught unawares if an underwater earthquake happened, or a volcano on some other small island erupted.

"Is it a volcano?"

Again, the boffin shook his head, then stopped. In the bottom right corner of the screen, a drone's camera showed nothing but the field. Leaning towards the screen, the man adjusted his glasses, then pulled away.

"Sir, you need to see this," he said, tapping the controls.

The image completely took over the screen and Pendleton cocked an eyebrow, unimpressed with what he was looking at. As he opened his mouth to yawn, Carruthers' voice crackled through the speakers. It was distorted and barely understandable.

"Repeat that," Pendleton said into the microphone as he watched the wobbling drone footage. Something felt off about it, but he couldn't quite put his finger on why. To him, it looked as if someone was rubbing Vaseline over the lens. The image was blurry, and he wasn't sure if it was a technical issue or had to do with whatever Carruthers was trying to say.

"… It's… Charles… Repeat… dinosaurs… charging… Charles!"

"Can you do something about this?" Pendleton said, gesturing to the speakers and microphone.

Quickly checking the sound equipment, the boffin shook his head before saying, "Audio is sending and receiving at optimal levels and frequencies. There's nothing wrong with the equipment." He pointed at the screen and said, "Maybe it's that."

Rolling his eyes, Pendleton didn't understand why the technician was so focused on a blurry camera. "It's a faulty drone. Bring it back for repairs if you're so worried about the damn thing, just find me those walking corpses!"

Hearing the threat in his voice, the technician's trembling hands pressed a couple of buttons and a panel next to him lit up.

As he looked at it, Pendleton grabbed the microphone and said as calmly as he could, "Carruthers, I can't hear a word of what you're saying. Please repeat and enunciate!" He placed the microphone back where it belonged, then focused on the boffin. "What is it now?"

"Sorry, sir, but the drone isn't malfunctioning. Look," the technician said and handed his boss a tablet.

Taking it, Pendleton saw the specifications and readings for the drone. The man was right, there was nothing wrong with it. So then, what was causing the strange image distortion?

Giving the tablet back, he stood next to the boffin and studied the screen. There was something very familiar about what he was seeing, and the more he stared at it, the more he realised it wasn't distortion.

"Get another drone on it," Pendleton said as the distortion sped up and now looked like a cloud. Next to him, the boffin nodded, then tapped a green button. "What is it?"

The young man sitting to his right chuckled nervously then said, "It looks like the sand wall from *The Mummy*. How great is that movie? Doesn't Brendan Fraser kick so much ass in it?"

That was it!

The inane pop culture reference did the trick, and Pendleton gasped. It was a cloud of dust and debris heading towards the compound. He'd never heard of or seen something like this and a part of him feared it.

What could be making it? he asked silently, but he already knew. It was an ingenious move and—

"Get everyone back inside," he said, tapping the boffin's shoulder. "They're not safe out there."

Frowning, the technician sent instructions to the various systems and a series of loud, almost deafening alarms sounded. The two men winced and covered their ears as the noise continued.

"Not in here!" Pendleton said, then sighed in relief the moment the hideous sound ended. Rubbing his hears, he muttered, "That was unpleasant."

His eyes found the screen, and he gasped. The image was now four separate squares, with different views from different drones. Each showed the dust cloud moving faster and faster, still heading towards the compound.

"What could make it?"

The speakers crackled, as Carruthers' panicking voice finally came through clearly. All he said was one word, but it was enough to make Charles Roy Pendleton step away from the control panel.

"*Stampede!*"

CHAPTER FORTY-SEVEN

The Ankylosaurus bellowed, the sound travelling across the wide-open field, and it shook its head. Large, flat feet thundered along the ground, kicking up dust and chunks of dirt as it ran. It roared again. This time it was higher in pitch and held a frantic tone.

The thick hide slammed into the body of a Stegosaurus. With its own bellow, the dino sped up. Sunlight reflected off the tail spikes that swung back and forth, carving grooves into the ground before sending chunks of earth into the sky.

Directly to its right was an Apatosaurus. The long neck stuck out in front of the heavy, lumbering body and bobbed up and down, but its eyes were wide and darted about in terror.

Just like the other fifteen dinosaurs stampeding towards Pendleton's compound. They didn't care where they were going, or what other species were with them. All they knew was that behind them was the most ferocious and dangerous predator known.

A Tyrannosaurus Rex!

A triceratops tripped, tumbling to the ground. Its massive paws fought to get it back up. The dinosaur shrieked, panicking as the T-Rex grew closer to it.

Behind them, keeping up as well as they could, were Sean Marshall, Walter Dillahunt, Frederica Alvaradejo, and Katherine Haywood. Their faces were red and each of them breathed hard. It was surprising how fast the lumbering-looking dinosaurs could move.

"Should we help it?" Alvaradejo asked, pointing at the still struggling triceratops. Its paws dug into the dirt and as it pushed itself off the ground, the dinosaur's weight became too much and it fell.

"How?" Marshall asked. The triceratops was another of his favourite dinosaur and there was a part of him that wanted to do whatever he could to get it moving again. But with the stench of the T-Rex shit covering him, it was impossible. "We don't have time for this. Keep moving."

He could see the concerned look on the Mexican's face and it surprised him, but also made sense at the same time. Most cold-blooded killers he met were usually loners, and had an affinity for animals more than humans. Like himself with dogs.

If they stopped, chances were they'd miss their window to use the stampeding dinos properly. Or get caught underfoot by more of the fleeing gigantic monsters.

No matter what, they couldn't stop.

On his right, Marshall saw Dillahunt. The Southerner was quiet, his face emotionless as he followed the dinosaurs. It was a little unsettling seeing him this quiet. Marshall expected him to be giddy with excitement that his plan was working.

"You okay, buddy?"

Dillahunt blinked before glancing at Marshall. Behind them, the triceratops bleated, panicking as another scent filled its nostrils. Hearing the sound, the Southerner turned and whistled, impressed with the sight.

"Damn, that boy can move!"

Turning his head, Marshall saw the dinosaur push itself off the ground, then use its tail to swipe at the snarling form of a raptor. The predator flew, crashing into another.

The triceratops twisted, standing upright, and it roared a challenge.

"Better than *Jurassic Park*," Alvaradejo said, then whooped for joy as the herbivore took off, charging towards the raptors that appeared from the tall grass behind them. "Should we be worried?"

Before he could answer, Marshall heard a growling. Looking to his left, beyond Dillahunt, he saw a group of raptors. It was impossible to count since they moved as one.

Like a flock of birds, he thought and shuddered.

"Not as much as those," Haywood said, gesturing to her right.

Following her gaze, the others saw more of the predators following them. They snarled and swiped their claws at the group of people, but never directly attacked. The stench of the Rex shit kept them at bay, and Marshall smiled at the one saving grace.

"Thank god this stuff has more than one use," Dillahunt said, cackling. His eyes were wide, and he glanced about, looking for incoming attacks.

"You good, soldier?"

Hearing the crack of Marshall's voice, the other man straightened, then nodded. His hands gripped the FN SCAR-L tightly, like it was a safety blanket. "I honestly didn't think this would work," he said, laughing again.

"Neither did I," Marshall said, his face splitting into a massive grin. He really didn't think it was going to work, but the fact the dinosaurs were stampeding, trampling everything underfoot and the raptors were keeping away from them, gave the Irishman hope they'd get off the island.

"I've got a question," Haywood said, her voice sounding hoarse from having to shout over the thundering footsteps and bellowing of the frightened animals up front. "How are we going to stop them from demolishing the compound and the escape vehicles?"

Marshall blinked, his smile vanishing. In his desire to come up with a plan, they'd forgotten to figure out how to slow or even steer the dinosaurs away from the actual building. He expected that once they broke through the fences, took out any of the hunters and defences, the dinos would turn on their own. Now, though, he wasn't so sure.

"Any ideas?" he asked Dillahunt, hoping the man had a way to stop the dinosaurs.

"For what?"

"Stopping them!" Alvaradejo shouted. "If anyone has an idea, they better speak now or forever hold their peace."

Confused by her words, Marshall followed her gaze. Between the dust, debris and dinosaurs, it was hard to see anything ahead of them. Frowning, he tried to see anything that wasn't the ass-end of a dinosaur, and laughed.

In the distance, he could see the faint outlines of the compound and cement structures that had to be towers. They were closer than he thought and a rush of adrenaline shot through his body.

This was it. They'd officially crossed the point of no return.

CHAPTER FORTY-EIGHT

"Think he could've built a bigger mansion?" Marshall said with a shake of his head as Pendleton's compound came into view.

Tall and statuesque, the central building's spires rose high above everything else, giving it the look of a grand old Victorian gothic mansion. Ostentatious was the word to describe it, but from what Marshall knew about Pendleton, it made sense.

A part of him expected to see gargoyles mounted on the corners of the roof. And with the knowledge that dinosaurs were still alive, it wouldn't be surprising to see the stone guardians come to life.

"Safeties off," Marshall said, smirking at his own childish imagination. His finger flipped his rifle's safety off and brought it up, ready to fire. "How are those raptors doing?"

Before he could answer, a low whoosh sounded, followed by a high-pitched whistling. It grew in volume, at an alarming speed, and Marshall tilted his head to the side slightly. It was a familiar sound.

"Incoming!" Dillahunt said a second before the ground exploded in front of the Ankylosaurus.

Its head was engulfed in fire, smoke and large heavy chunks of rock and the dinosaur shrieked. Rising into the air, the stench of burning flesh wafted from it and the dinosaur whimpered before going still.

"Rockets," Marshall mumbled as he dusted himself off. Looking about, he saw the other three were fine, then turned his attention to the front and gasped.

The dinosaurs still charged. None noticed the death of the Aankylosaurus or even the explosion. Their fear of the T-Rexes behind them kept pushing them on.

As always, fear was the greatest motivator.

"They're launching again!" Alvaradejo shouted as the roar of another missile firing filled the air.

Marshall had an idea. It was the only thing they could do at the moment if they wanted to survive. "Slow down! Let the dinos take the brunt of the attacks."

A second later, the ground exploded again in a devastating blast of destruction. This time it was in front of a Brachiosaurus, and the long-necked dinosaur barely noticed the flames. The animal's small head swayed back and forth and it bellowed, but kept moving.

"How many of those things you think they got?" Dillahunt said, using the slower pace to breathe deeply. "And is this the best idea with those fuckers out there?"

Marshall knew what he meant. The raptors wouldn't wait forever. Rex stench or not, they'd eventually go for the kill. That meant they needed to keep moving, but Marshall wasn't sure what the best course of action was.

"Zig-zag," Alvaradejo said, making a slashing motion with her hand. "Even if those *pendejos* keep firing missiles, they won't hit us. We use the dinosaurs as cover. *Si?*"

All Marshall could do was smile and nod at the woman's suggestion. It made sense and perfectly illustrated why a team was better in most incursions than a single man.

A tracer round shot past Marshall's face, the heat distortion startling him, and he flinched. "What the fuck?"

Looking up, he saw more of the bullets tear through the air. From the rate of fire, he figured they were Gatling guns, or high-powered machine guns. Either way, they needed to be more careful now. Even zig-zagging could result in their demise.

"Stay low and alert," Marshall said. The herd of stampeding dinosaurs was fifty metres ahead of them, with the gap increasing. If they didn't want the raptors to attack them, they needed to move fast.

Marshall was glad for the missiles and rapid-firing guns. They cleared the air of the dust and dirt kicked up by the dinosaurs. In front of them, he could see the bullets slam into thick hides, sending ripples along the impact point, but the dinosaurs ignored it.

He didn't fully understand how stampedes worked and made a mental note to ask Dillahunt about the mechanics later.

A missile smacked into the armour plating of an Ankylosaurus, bouncing off the side of the animal. It spun through the air, performing a strange cartwheel before thudding to the ground behind the group of people.

Turning, Marshall saw a raptor leap towards it, talons extended, ready for the kill.

It landed on top of the device and as the long-curved toe claws pierced the casing, the missile exploded, disintegrating the dinosaur in a ball of flame.

"Must go faster," Marshall said as the other raptors bellowed their rage. "We've got incoming, and they are pissed!" He didn't want to look, the eardrum-shredding howls chasing after them. It was clear what was happening, but out of the corner of his eye, he saw Dillahunt glance behind him.

"Jesuschristoncrutches!" the Southerner said, turning to face the front. "Those beasties are certainly miffed."

Now's the time he goes for understatement? Marshall thought as, behind them, the raptors swarmed.

It was impossible to tell how many of the deadly prehistoric monsters there were. There were more than thirty, that was for sure, and Marshall felt his legs pump harder than before as a feeling of dread filled his stomach.

They needed a miracle.

CHAPTER FORTY-NINE

The sensation reminded Marshall of standing next to a stack of subwoofers at a concert and he felt it in his gut. His innards bounced in time with a consistent, deep, unperceivable sound and he felt queasy.

Looking to his left then right, he saw the others slow, then speed up again as an infrasonic rumbling took over the area. None of them had heard anything like this before and a primal emotion, long dormant, woke with a new drive.

To get away from the sound.

"What the fuck is that?" Dillahunt asked, trying to be heard over the sound. Behind them, the raptors slowed, their heads sniffing the air as the sound washed over them.

Marshall didn't know what it was, but he was positive there was one who did. Turning to his right, he saw Haywood shake her head. The woman's eyes were wide and filled with abject terror. She definitely knew what the source was.

"Must be some croc," Dillahunt said, answering his own question. He shook his head, trying to rid himself of the pressure that filled his ears.

Watching the man's movement, Marshall realised he felt the same thing and squeezed his nostrils shut. Taking a breath, he blew, trying to pop them. Instead, all he did was make himself dizzy, and he gasped for air.

"¡Detente!"

Hearing Spanish, Marshall looked at Alvaradejo. The Mexican slid to a stop and pointed ahead of her. Following the extended arm, Marshall dug his heels into the dirt.

The herd of dinosaurs ahead of them stood motionless. Their heads darted about as they sniffed the air. It was a strange reaction, completely unexpected, and Marshall's grip on the HK416 tightened.

"What the fuck is it?" he asked as the rumbling intensified. He looked at Haywood again, waiting for an answer, but all the woman did was stand, eyes wide and mouth open. "Haywood! What the fuck is that?"

With a frustrated shake of her head, Alvaradejo turned and slapped the other woman hard. The sound made the men wince, and they watched the survivor stumble out of her stupor.

"Fuck!" Haywood said, rubbing her cheek. Looking around, her hands trembled, and she glanced behind her before snapping back to the others. "We need to get out of here, it's going to be—"

The deafening squeals of terror that came from the dinosaurs drowned out the rest of her words. Ahead of them, the herbivores reared up, heads swaying from side to side as they cried, then slammed their feet into the ground before barrelling forwards again.

Whatever was causing the sound, it was more frightening than the T-Rex stench that emanated off the people.

"Fuck me," Marshall said before looking behind him.

To their rear, the raptors were in a frenzy. A series of roars, howls, and shrieks came from them as they clawed at each other, scrambling over one another as panic drove them crazy. Soon, they'd feel the urge to charge, fleeing the terrible sound, and Marshall could tell they were in the way.

"Run!" he bellowed before chasing after the lead dinosaurs. All thoughts of the mansion dashed from his mind. Now Marshall cared about only one thing.

Surviving the double stampede.

Feet pounding the ground, he vaguely heard Haywood's scream, "It's a mutha-fucking T-Rex!"

CHAPTER FIFTY

"It's the Tyrannosaurus Rex!"

The technician's voice was a whisper to Charles Roy Pendleton. His eyes were completely focused on the screens, and the approaching dinosaurs.

"Charles, did you hear me?" the boffin asked as the mansion trembled, caught in the middle of an earthquake and a tsunami. There was nothing either of them could do to stop the dinosaur stampede, except get out of the way. "That's the Rex!"

Pendleton shook his head. It was a slight movement and the young, glasses-wearing man scoffed. He couldn't believe it; the Rex never came to this part of the island. Its range was beyond the mountain range that split the island in two. There had to be a rational reason for its sudden appearance.

"Are they clear?"

"Of course they are. But the projections show the dinos are heading right for us! They're not going to be able to change course fast enough. Especially not with the Rex whipping them up into a frenzy."

The technician was right, and any other day Pendleton would've given him a raise and a hefty bonus. But right now, he didn't need the obvious stated. He needed answers, or plans. Everything was falling apart around him and there was nobody to blame except for himself.

"Are you sure it's the Rex?"

"Of course I'm fucking sure! What else would it be?" the technician said. He shook Pendleton by the shoulders and said, "Charles, we need to get the fuck out of here. Right now! Those things are going to demolish this place. You don't want to be here for that."

He was right. Pendleton knew this, but he couldn't move. *It couldn't be the T-Rex. It just couldn't be.*

"What would bring the Rex here?"

"The fucking stampede! That many dinos moving as one would bring any large carnivore to the area." The technician tapped the control panel. "Shit. All the raptors are behind them. Charles, for the love of God, we've got to get moving. Please!"

All Charles Roy Pendleton could do was wave the man way. "Go, join the others. I'll finish this."

Before the boffin could say anything else, Pendleton shoved him towards one of the doors. If he took it, the moustached man knew he'd get to the underground bunker Carruthers should've led the others to. Once the stampede was over, they'd be able to get off the island and leave the dinosaurs there to do what they did best.

Hearing the man's footsteps fade away, Pendleton stepped up to the console. He touched a couple of controls lightly, sending a command to the drones to return to their bases. Once that was done, he brought up the perimeter fence cameras.

The images trembled and flickered, static cutting in as the signal's strength fluctuated. That was to be expected, and Pendleton activated the electric fences. Sparks flew and he smiled.

Not done yet, he thought as he pressed another couple of buttons in sequence, then watched as cement barriers rose in between the fences. The added weight and stopping power mixed with the ten thousand volts of the fences would slow anything down, if not stop them outright.

Turning on his heel, Pendleton stared at the opulently decorated room and smiled sadly. His legacy was this, a ruined family and an island full of dangerous creatures. It was the ultimate joke, and he laughed.

His back to the screens, Pendleton couldn't see the charging dinosaurs grow closer and closer to his home, away from home. If he did, he'd have turned and fled, leaving the others to deal with the fallout themselves.

Instead, the man closed his eyes as the shaking of his mansion escalated and paintings, light fixtures and pieces of plaster tumbled to the floor.

An earth-shattering crack sounded as the first of the dinosaurs slammed into the fence.

CHAPTER FIFTY-ONE

"Don't fucking stop!" Marshall shouted, pushing the others on. It didn't matter that the fence was destroyed, bent at an almost perpendicular angle to the ground. Or that chunks of cement littered the ground, resembling boulders.

There was no reason to stop and stare at the downed dinosaurs, impaled on thick wire or killed by impossibly high voltages.

What mattered was they make it inside the mansion.

Pendleton's opulent, gothic place of residence still stood. Yes, it had been damaged by the dinosaurs, but whoever built it knew what they were doing.

Up close now, the mansion seemed even more over-the-top than before. Strange angles gave it the appearance of being out of place, and Marshall felt as if he'd stumbled into a strange horror tale.

"Where is everyone?" Haywood asked, clambering over a section of wrecked fence. The cement rocked from her weight, and extending her arms, she steadied it before dropping. "There should be crazies out here."

"Crazies?" Dillahunt said, mimicking her voice. "Lady, I doubt the craziest person out there would stand in the way of that," he said, pointing to an Apatosaurus lying on its side.

Marshall watched Alvaradejo go over to it. She crouched next to the animal's head, then reached out and petted it. Moving his eyes down the length of the thick neck, he saw thick strands of cable and wire sticking out of its side.

It must've impaled itself crashing through the barrier, he reasoned.

The dinosaur wheezed, blood bubbling from its mouth. It didn't have long and a part of him wanted to join the Mexican in saying goodbye. But he didn't want to intrude on something solemn and instead, turned to face Haywood.

"How the fuck is that thing still standing?"

The woman shook her head before brushing strands of red hair off her face. Sweat covered her, but with the dust and detritus from the crash, she looked like a ghost and Marshall realised they all must look a sight.

"What happened to the raptors?" Dillahunt asked, pointing to the air.

Turning to face him, Marshall was struck by the horrible realisation that they were now alone in the ruined courtyard of the compound. He couldn't see any of the dinosaurs, dead or alive, including the raptors, and he shuddered from the stillness.

"That's not the problem," Haywood said, dropping her voice to above a whisper. "What about the Rex?"

Looking at her, Marshall opened his mouth, then closed it. He didn't notice the eerie silence. Like most people, he was too reliant on his eyes and in this situation, ignoring his other senses was a surefire way of getting killed.

"We need to get moving," he said, gesturing towards the front door. Turning to Dillahunt, Marshall said, "Get Frederica."

"With pleasure," Dillahunt said, a massive grin on his face. Without saying another word, he turned and jogged over to the fallen dinosaur and the solitary woman mourning its death.

Marshall watched the two, and a small smile crept across his lips. Even though they were killers and wanted by the authorities for countless crimes, he felt a fondness for them that only came from battle.

"I sometimes forget what magnificent animals they are," Haywood said softly next to him. Watching Alvaradejo say goodbye to the prehistoric animal was calming and acted like a release after the running.

But it couldn't go on forever.

Nodding, Marshall turned to the woman. His eyes widened, and he shoved her out of the way as his rifle snapped up and he squeezed the trigger.

A man, eyes wide in shock, staggered as bullets shredded his body. He collapsed, dead before he hit the ground, and blood oozed from his wounds.

"We've got company!" Marshall barked as a group of men appeared on either side of the compound. *Underground bunkers*, he thought, and cursed himself for getting distracted. "Controlled shots! Don't waste your ammo and head for the doors."

Not bothering to see if the other two heard his orders, Marshall shoved Haywood towards the dark double doors. "Get inside," he said, his thumb flicking the rate of fire switch to auto.

Squeezing the trigger, he moved the HK146's barrel back and forth, watching tiny eruptions of blood spurt from the approaching men's chests. He wasn't worried about killing them.

He needed to buy enough time for the others to get inside safely.

Behind him, he heard the war-cries of Dillahunt and Alvaradejo, followed by the roar of their weapons.

"Get moving!" Marshall shouted over his shoulder while at the same time counting the number of men stumbling out of the wreckage, fumbling with their weapons and, in general, acting like rank amateurs.

Their behaviour made him shake his head. If he knew they were this incompetent, firing wildly at him and hitting nothing, he wouldn't have been as worried. The only thing he was concerned about was the number of men inside the mansion itself.

At least thirty, Marshall finished counting the men trying to surround them. He could hear the others closing in on him. If both Alvaradejo and Dillahunt caught up to him, then they'd have a better chance of making it.

The baboon-like shriek of a raptor froze everyone. As the seconds ticked by, more of the piss-inducing calls sounded, and Marshall shook his head. *Why couldn't they catch a break?*

"Run," Haywood's voice was like a starter gun in his ear. That was the only move to make, and Marshall just hoped they could make it before the killer dinosaurs got there.

CHAPTER FIFTY-TWO

"You heard the lady," Marshall said, squeezing the trigger once more. The hunters ducked to the ground, and he kept his finger pressed on the piece of metal until the gun clicked empty. "Reloading," he said, ejecting the spent magazine.

Turning, he saw Haywood standing in front of the doors. She had one of the large, ornately carved slabs of wood open and was beckoning for the others to hurry. That was incentive enough for him, and Marshall ran towards it.

"What the fuck is that?" he heard one hunter ask. The question stopped Marshall, who, turning, felt the ground crumble below him.

Standing on top of a dead Stegosaurus' head was a compy. The small, green, bird-like dinosaur chirped as it looked at the group of men and the surrounding carnage. Its pitch-black eyes scanned the area, and it bobbed up and down on its hind legs.

Backing away slowly, Marshall said to Dillahunt and Alvaradejo, "Move slow. If that thing calls for re-enforcements, we're fucked."

"That thing's dangerous?" Dillahunt said, chuckling as the small dinosaur pecked at the flesh under it. Peeling a layer of skin from the body, the compy ate it, making a small slurping sound mixed with a purr.

Marshall nodded and gestured for them to keep moving. His instincts were to run, but doing so would alert the dinosaur and if that happened, they would definitely be up shit creek.

As the thought crossed his mind, one of the hunters stepped forward, his large heavy boot cracking cement. The sound was louder than an explosion, catching the compy's attention instantly.

Lifting its head, the small dinosaur made a pulsating clicking. As its strange song continued, what sounded like fifty similar sounds responded, and Marshall trembled.

It was calling for back-up.

"It's cute," a different hunter, a young man wearing glasses, said, stepping towards the dinosaur. His weapon, a double-barrel shotgun, thudded to the ground as he got closer to the compy.

Watching the area behind the small dinosaur, Marshall spotted more of the ferocious, ravenous monsters hopping, scrambling over the destroyed fences and barriers. His eyes darted from the dinos to the other men, and he shook his head. They hadn't seen the rest approaching, which meant he and the others had a chance.

"You're almost there," Haywood said, voice tight but encouraging, and Marshall fought the urge to run.

"How much farther?"

"Twenty metres or so."

Marshall nodded. They could make it!

He didn't give a flying rat's ass about the others. If they were devoured, so be it, and if any made it to the bunkers, good for them. His focus was on getting inside, finding Pendleton, then getting off the godforsaken island.

Moving his eyes back to the hunter, he saw the man clamber up the side of the dead dinosaur. His hands gripped folds of skin as he pulled himself up towards the compy.

Don't do it, he thought as his mind brought forth the image of Beaumont doing the exact same thing. The hunter's fate would be the same, first a taste and then the swarm would strip his bones clean.

"Once it happens," Marshall said, "make for the door. Don't turn back or anything."

"Once what happens?" Alvaradejo asked. Her voice trembled slightly and Marshall could feel nervousness radiating off her.

The hunter reached a hand out, crooking his finger as if he was calling a cat or dog. In front of him, the compy leaned forward and chirruped. The small mouth opened, and it sniffed the air, taking in the man's scent.

An orange blur slammed into the hunter. Bright red blood splattered the ground, painting the compy and area as the man wailed in pain. Large curved claws tore at his stomach, while sharp teeth shredded his face.

The compy screeched in protest, then leapt for the raptor eating its meal.

Without warning, a green and brown swarm of compies appeared. All snarled and attacked the feeding raptor. The dinosaur bellowed and began defending itself, the talon hands and toes swiping out at the smaller dinos.

But there were too many of them and in seconds, the smaller dinosaurs covered it.

"Hawthorne!" another hunter cried out and lifted his twin Desert Eagle pistols. The guns cracked with each shot, the large calibre bullets shredding the compies with each hit.

Tiny bodies somersaulted into the air as blood and viscera spread, covering everything in a disgusting paste. With each shot, more compies appeared, taking the place of the fallen. Within seconds, the raptor and hunter's carcasses, pieces of tattered flesh and fabric dangled from the bones remained and the dinos turned to the other hunters.

"Go," Marshall said, turning to run as the pounding of feet and snorting announced the arrival of the raptors.

Snarls and growls filled the air as the larger predators launched themselves at the hunters. The crack of guns firing and men screaming in terror followed the three as they got closer to the doors and Haywood.

"Drop!" Haywood shouted as she lifted an AK-47. Marshall didn't see her take it back on the plane, but he was glad she was armed.

Squeezing the trigger, Haywood shook from the recoil. Her arms went up, forced by the power of the rifle, and she screamed in fright.

Diving to the ground, Marshall felt the bullets fly over him and rolling onto his back, he saw three raptors tumble to the ground. Blood oozed from the fresh wounds that dotted their bodies, and he smiled at the sight of the light fading from their eyes.

Getting to his feet, he heard a shrill bellowing as the jaws of a raptor closed around Haywood's arm.

Before he could react, the dinosaur dragged the screaming woman away from them, her voice cracking as she struggled to free herself from the powerful beast.

"Haywood!" Marshall shouted as he lifted his gun. Staring down the sights, he watched in disbelief as the raptor dropped the woman then placed a heavy clawed foot on her chest.

He couldn't see what the woman said, but as Dillahunt dragged him across the threshold, Marshall saw a fountain of blood spurt high into the air. An instant later, a sickening crunch filled his ears, and he knew it.

Haywood was dead.

CHAPTER FIFTY-THREE

The moment the large, heavy duty oak doors slammed shut behind him, Marshall drove his fist into the wood and swore.

"She was supposed to make it!" he said as he used the image of Haywood's fear-stricken face to push him on.

If he couldn't save her, then he'd avenge her.

"That's upsetting," Dillahunt said, and, turning around, Marshall fought the urge to puke as his eyes took in the troubling sight.

On either side of the long hallway, taxidermied people stood guard. Their lifeless eyes stared blankly at nothing, as their faces were forever frozen in screams of pain, fear, or rage. A few of the lifelike statues held weapons, but it was obvious they were empty.

Slowly, the three began walking down the length of the room. Alvaradejo made the sign of the cross and offered a prayer in Spanish before turning and doing the same to the others.

"Why would anyone do this?" Marshall's voice was hushed as they kept moving.

Speakers crackled and Charles Roy Pendleton's voice boomed. "Why, you ask? It's not a question of why, Mister Marshall, but why not?"

Hearing the man's voice, their weapons snapped up, and they scanned the area. Another ten metres and the hallway opened up to two side rooms and an enormous staircase.

Moving past the 'guards', they saw decapitated heads, stuffed and mounted on the walls like trophies. Looking at the faces and the engraved plates under them, Marshall felt the urge to burn the place down. It would be easy to do. All he needed would be fuel and an open flame.

"I asked you a question! Why wouldn't you want to do this? This island is my home! Nobody knows it exists apart from my family and a select few. Oh, those men out there aren't like me. By the way, my kudos for making it this far. I wasn't expecting that. But to be honest, I'd grown bored with the hunts."

"Anybody else want to make Pendleton suffer?" Dillahunt asked as he checked the current magazine loaded into the FN SCAR-L. His face was ashen grey as he tried not to stare too long at the rows and rows of vacant eyes.

Both Marshall and Alvaradejo nodded. There was no room to let the hunters or Pendleton live.

Everyone had to die.

"Think the dinos will get in?" Alvaradejo asked. Her voice was dead, completely emotionless, and her eyes looked the same as when Marshall first met her.

A banging on the large door behind them was the perfect answer. Muffled screams and begging for sanctuary came through and the three heard snarling, followed by gunfire.

The raptors and compies were winning.

"See, us Pendletons are the top one percent of the rich. But after investing in technology, medicine, war and humanity, what else was there to do? You see the dilemma?" Pendleton's voice was close now.

Switching the rate of fire to full-auto, both Marshall and Dillahunt readied themselves. Next to him, he felt Alvaradejo check her guns as well. They were ready to end it.

"You're being very rude, not answering me," Pendleton said with the tone of a petulant child. "I think you'll be fed to the dinos after all. You're not good enough to be put on display with the rest of my trophies."

Exiting the hallway, the three ignored the doors on either side of them. Pendleton waited on the staircase, a grandiose place for a fight. The only thing that had Marshall worried was the weapons he'd be armed with.

Hugging the walls, they slowly exited the hallway, feeling warmth from the soft lights that bathed the foyer in faint candlelight. The staircase was opulent, stretching off in two directions at the midpoint, reminding Marshall of the sort seen in *Gone with the Wind*.

"Took you long enough," Pendleton said with a disappointed shake of his head. He sat on the stairs, a D'arcy Echols hunting rifle resting on his lap.

"*¡Que se joda este cabrón!*" Alvaradejo snarled before stepping forward. Automatically, her eyes narrowed as her arms brought both guns up.

Pendleton clapped his hands. "Bravo! But do you think I'd make it that easy?"

Before the woman could pull the triggers, their target held up a remote control and pressed a big red button.

Behind them, the door unlocked itself with a loud click. Marshall and Dillahunt spun, keeping their rifles at the ready, and watched in terror as the door swung open with a soft groan. Neither of the men thought

Pendleton would have full control of the building, and Marshall cursed himself for making a rookie mistake.

This cunt really needs to die, he thought as the door slammed against the wall. Bloodied, terrified men fell across the threshold as the dinos flooded the building.

Dropping to his knee, Marshall squeezed the trigger of his rifle in short, controlled bursts. He didn't care if he killed the dinosaurs, he just needed to keep them from getting closer.

Next to him, he could hear Dillahunt firing, but unlike him, he was holding the trigger down and sweeping his weapon back and forth, a joy-filled exaltation on his lips.

"Now, how about that!" Marshall heard Pendleton say before vanishing up the stairs. A series of gunshots followed the fleeing man and, once again, Alvaradejo cursed.

Marshall opened his mouth, then went silent. The sub-sonic rumbling rocked the building and his innards. Unlike before, this time it felt like it was right on top of him.

"Follow Pendleton!" he barked the moment he saw the raptors and compies freeze. Marshall was glad the sound affected the dinosaurs. He didn't want to deal with them as well as the fleeing madman.

Tapping Dillahunt's shoulder, he turned and started up the stairs. He knew Alvaradejo was already following him and once he got to the same spot that Pendleton sat on, he turned and began firing.

That was the other man's cue to move his ass.

Hurrying up the stairs, the three heard the roaring of the raptors drown out the pounding of feet. The other doors opened and even more armed men appeared. A bloodbath was going to ensue, but they knew the dinosaurs would win.

Superior numbers.

CHAPTER FIFTY-FOUR

Marshall's foot slammed into the double doors. It was the only locked room on the upper floors and had to be where Pendleton hid. The wood groaned and buckled but didn't give.

With a frustrated grunt, he brought his foot up again, ready to deliver another blow.

"We don't have time for this," Dillahunt said with a shake of his head. Before Marshall could react, the man lifted his FN SCAR-L, aimed at the lock and handle, then squeezed the trigger.

The bullets shredded the wood surrounding the antique-looking handle. With a satisfied chuckle, Dillahunt released the trigger, and the lock tumbled to the floor. Using the weapon, he nudged Marshall out of the way before delivering his own devastating blow.

With a crash that sounded like bones snapping, the doors flew open and the three rushed into the room.

Marshall and Dillahunt took the lead, using a standard breeching formation while Alvaradejo brought up the rear. Each of them kept their faces emotionless. Their focus was on the man who was to blame for all of this.

"Nice office," Marshall heard Dillahunt mutter, and he had to admit, it was impressive, but they didn't have time to admire it.

In front of them, massive windows opened out to a balcony that overlooked more of the island and then the water. Marshall could see what he hoped was the helipad below and he smiled.

They had an escape route.

Scanning the room, he saw a bank of monitors. The images were security camera feeds of the destruction, chaos and carnage going on inside the rest of the building; the dinos were decimating the other hunters and staff. Their powerful jaws made arms and legs seem like noodles while the long-curved toe-claw sliced through flesh, spilling more blood and internal organs over the pristine floor.

At the same time, the compies, as one, slammed into man and beast. Their teeth and claws made short work of skin, muscle and sinews, leaving carcasses in their wake.

The terrified men slipped in the spilt viscera as they tried to escape the gnashing teeth and sharp claws. It was a smorgasbord for the dinosaurs, who looked actually happy with the feast they'd been given.

And even though the bloodshed on display was riveting, Marshall had one question. Where the fuck was Charles Roy Pendleton?

A wood panel behind him cracked, bullets smashing into it. Splinters exploded, covering the stunned man, who dropped to the floor. On either side of him, he saw Alvaradejo and Dillahunt in the same positions.

"Why the fuck can't we get the drop on this asshole?" Dillahunt growled as he looked about, trying to find a line of sight.

On the other side of Marshall, Alvaradejo said, "Because you two suck at this! Just distract him, okay?"

Not waiting for an answer, the woman rolled away from them. Both men watched as she vanished behind a couch, then looked at each other in disbelief. Above them, the rapid fire of two six-shooters decimating wood panelling told them Pendleton was still focused on them.

"Think he'll play whack-a-mole?"

Marshall frowned in confusion. Then, a second later, he grinned and nodded his head. It was an ingenious idea and perfect to keep Pendleton busy. All they had to do was make sure they didn't get winged. "I'll go first," Marshall said with a grin.

Gripping his rifle close to his chest, he counted the shots fired. Once he knew Pendleton was reloading, he'd pop up and fire.

"We don't have to play!" he said with a giggle. "Just wait for him to reload and then take him out."

Pouting, Dillahunt said, "It was a good idea, anyway."

Marshall nodded and chuckled. It was a good idea, but it made more sense for them to wait it out. Even if Pendleton hid to reload, they could still fire at him. As long as he didn't notice the woman, he could keep firing.

The room went silent, and the two nodded. It was time.

Scrambling to his feet, Marshall's HK416 snapped up and fired. Bullets sped through the air, hitting nothing but the windows. The glass shuddered and cracked, but didn't break.

Pendleton dropped behind the large, expensive looking desk for cover.

Next to him, Dillahunt also fired, though he still pouted.

"You've got to be shitting me," Marshall said as his body trembled again. It was even more intense than before, and he was positive that his teeth would fall out.

Steadying himself against the couch, Dillahunt groaned. The entire room shook as if it was caught in an earthquake. The panelling cracked, then fell to the floor while the screens flickered before exploding from the infrasonic sound waves.

"Now you're dead!"

The men barely heard Pendleton's voice above the fear-inducing sound. Looking, they saw their target with Alvaradejo in a headlock. The woman struggled, but the S&W Model 500's barrel buried in the back of her head kept her from going berserk.

"Drop the guns!" Pendleton barked over the deafening rumbling. His eyes darted about, making sure he was safe, and his body trembled.

"Let her go!" Marshall bellowed, then gasped in shock.

Seeing the man's face, Pendleton turned to look behind him. His voice cracked as he screamed in terror, releasing Alvaradejo.

She barely had enough time to dive out of the way as the window and balcony exploded, destroyed by a large tooth-filled mouth that cut through the structure like it was butter. Shards of glass, wood, tiling, and wiring crashed into the screaming man.

The massive mouth of a Tyrannosaurus Rex opened and, in one smooth motion, gripped Charles Roy Pendleton around his torso. Blood exploded from his mouth and he went limp as the king of the dinosaurs devoured him.

CHAPTER FIFTY-FIVE

The dinosaur's eyes focused on the three people gaping at it. Blood and chunks of flesh oozed from between its teeth and the rumbling continued, its lower jaw and the throat vibrating as it pulled its massive head back and shook it.

Even more debris rained down from it.

"Did you see that?" Dillahunt shouted as he pointed at the terrifying beast.

Marshall had seen it, but that wasn't his focus. Behind the monstrous body, he could plainly see the helipad and an Airbus H130 helicopter sitting on it.

"Talk later. Right now, move ya ass!"

He shoved the man and woman back out the door as the T-Rex snarled, then crashed into the building, focused completely on the fleeing snacks.

Careening through the building, Marshall kept looking ahead, making sure there were no raptors and then behind them. Though it wouldn't matter if the massive dinosaur was right behind them or not, it was bigger than he expected and more terrifying than the movies made out.

Large cracks snaked out, chasing them as the beast forced its way through the man-made construct.

The shrieks of the raptors told them they were close to the staircase and the moment they rounded a corner and saw them, both men lifted their automatic rifles and fired.

Bullets sprayed, penetrating flesh, shredding organs and cracking bones as they pushed forward.

They didn't know which way to go, but Marshall was positive there was a door out back. There was no way they could survive going out the front then work their way around to the back and helicopter.

It was out the back or nothing.

"Is it still behind us?" Marshall grunted before slipping in offal. A shock of pain ran through him and he knew he pulled a muscle, but it didn't matter. They had to keep moving.

The staircase wobbled, then bounced as the T-Rex appeared at the top of it. Its eyes scanned the area, and it growled at the sight of the raptors.

"Yes!" Alvaradejo answered Marshall's question as the smaller dinosaurs howled at the sight of the massive dinosaur. Then, as one, they swarmed towards it, leaping onto its flank; they dug their claws and sharp teeth into the thick flesh. The attack caused the T-Rex to snarl and whip its head around, tying to dislodge the smaller animals.

It's going to fall! Marshall thought at the same time he spotted the kitchen and leading out of it, a path to the helipad.

They could make it!

The mass of dinosaurs twisted as the T-Rex's foot smashed through the stairs. Its weight was too great, and it fell, crashing through the wood and cement structures.

The impact and jagged edges of wood shredded the raptors on its side. Others jumped at the last minute, but the force at which the monstrously sized dino fell, destroying everything as it careened towards the lower levels.

"This place isn't going to last much longer!" Marshall bellowed as around them, the walls buckled and cracked. Any second now, the mansion would collapse and there was no way he or the others would be caught in it.

In the kitchen, Marshall saw three raptors. They were rummaging through the fridge and pantry. Lifting his rifle, he squeezed the trigger, sending one of the beasts to the ground.

The other two, hearing the shot, looked up then roared.

Before either dinosaur could charge, Dillahunt's FN SCAR-L bellowed, shredding the prehistoric monsters.

Without a second thought, the three leapt over the corpses before slamming through the door as Pendleton's home caved in on itself with a deafening roar.

CHAPTER FIFTY-SIX

A cloud of dust and debris engulfed the trio as they tumbled to the ground. Closing their eyes and holding their breaths, they waited for the wind to clear the area.

Marshall coughed and groaned as he felt the breeze gently caress him. It was soothing, but the moment he felt it, he looked at the other two.

Dillahunt sat up, face frozen in shock as his mouth moved silently. It looked as if he was trying to figure out everything he'd seen.

"You okay?" he asked Alvaradejo. The woman was curled up in a ball, arms covering her head for protection. Marshall reached out and tapped her shoulder before saying, "Come on, we have to keep moving."

Slowly, the woman looked up from under her arms, saw the darkening sky, and smiled. Dusting herself down, her eyes spotted the waiting helicopter. "*¡Gracias madre virgen!*"

Marshall knew how she felt and if he was religious, he'd offer a prayer of his own. "We need to keep moving. I don't want any other surprises today."

"Can you believe it?" Dillahunt finally said, as the three stood and dusted themselves off. "Pendleton was killed by a T-fucking-Rex! That's all levels of awesome."

Nodding, Marshall headed towards the helipad. His eyes took in the area; not only was there the helicopter and fuel pumps but also a small dock that had a couple of frigates moored. This was how they got their food and other supplies. It was quite an operation, and he was proud they had dismantled it.

"We should hurry," he said, checking his weapons. Somehow, he had kept hold of his HK416 and his last two magazines. Without another word, he started jogging towards the helicopter.

He didn't worry about the other two. Marshall knew they were right behind him and as he got closer to the area, he felt a smile appear. They were finally free and able to do what they wanted!

Of course, he knew he was going back to work. But there was a part of him that wanted to go back to the UK and re-join the service. Working with Dillahunt and Alvaradejo had reignited his joy for squad work.

Brody's going to be pissed, he thought with a chuckle, then frowned. Once back, he'd have to take care of that betrayal. After that, he had no idea what he'd do. It didn't matter, though. Working as a bounty hunter wasn't permanent.

So, what was stopping him?

The answer was straightforward: nobody but Sean Marshall. That did it. The moment they got back to civilisation, he'd re-enlist and pick up right where he left off.

"Who's flying that thing?"

The question broke Marshall's train of thought, and he looked from the helicopter to the others. It was a simple question, but one he hadn't taken into consideration.

"I can," Alvaradejo said, holding up her hand. "My bosses need someone who can handle anything."

Both men nodded, not bothering to ask any follow-up questions. They watched Alvaradejo jog to the stairs leading up to the helicopter. She took them two at a time and the moment she cleared them, she set about inspecting the aircraft.

"She's an interesting one." Dillahunt's voice was filled with admiration and worry.

Patting the man's arm, Marshall chuckled, then said, "You're both free of your past lives, remember? Do what you want and be with who you want."

It was corny advice, but made sense in their current situation. Before the other man could say anything, the Mexican's voice floated through the air. "Get your *pinche* asses up here and help me get this thing loose!"

Looking up at her, they could see Alvaradejo pointing at the thick straps that held the Airbus H130 in place on the helipad. It was standard practice, a precaution to make sure it wouldn't be swept away or stolen.

"You heard the lady," Marshall said before heading for the stairs. He took them two at a time and within seconds was helping the woman free the helicopter.

Looking up, he saw Dillahunt remove the straps from the rotor blades and as he smiled, the infrasonic rumbling started again.

CHAPTER FIFTY-SEVEN

"You've got to be fucking kidding." Marshall sighed in disbelief as the three people stared at the smoking ruins of the compound. The moment they heard the rumbling, they ceased their activities and turned to stare in horror.

The rubble trembled, then, with an almighty roar, the T-Rex exploded from the wreckage.

Large, ugly scratches and gouges dotted its flesh with the dead bodies of the raptors still clinging to it. Its left eye was a puckered bloodied mess and one of the tiny arms swayed. Its movements were jerky as the T-Rex shook its body, trying to dislodge the carcasses, and pieces of wood and plaster impaled in it.

"How is that even possible?" Dillahunt asked and even though the others had the same question race into their minds, none could answer it.

The only thing Marshall could think of was staying still. But so far, everything *Jurassic Park* had taught him was wrong. "We need to move. Now. Doesn't matter about the Rex. We have to get airborne before it spots us."

The words were barely out of his mouth when a low raspy-sounding growl came from the dinosaur. Looking at it, he saw the one good eye staring back at them.

It had already spotted them.

"Freddie, get us ready. Walter, let's go. Yeah?"

Orders received, the man and woman nodded, then took off. Alvaradejo quickly jumped into the pilot's seat and checked the various gauges covering the panel. She placed her feet on the pedals and checked the rear rotor and flaps. They moved with ease, and she chuckled.

So far, so good.

As she continued her pre-flight check of the helicopter, Marshall and Dillahunt hurried to undo the remaining straps. As he fought with the release, Marshall looked up in time to see the large carnivorous dinosaur stalking towards them. Its head lowered like a battering ram, keeping its one good eye on them.

"Must go faster," Marshall heard himself say, then giggled childishly. It wasn't the right time for such a comment, but he couldn't help himself.

The final strap released, Marshall waved at Alvaradejo, who nodded, strapped herself in and switched the ignition on. With a mechanical groan, the rotors spun slowly. Even though they needed to be airborne sooner rather than later, Alvaradejo knew better than to rush the start-up sequence.

"What now?" he heard Dillahunt shout at him while gesturing at the approaching T-Rex.

Marshall knew what he was getting at, but there was only one thing left to do. "Get on!" he bellowed, shoving the other man towards the side of the helicopter.

Dillahunt crashed into it, slamming his head against a covered cylinder. Rubbing the back of his cranium, the man clambered up into the cargo hold and pulled away the tarp. A wide grin appeared on his face and he kissed the mounted GE M134 Minigun.

Seeing the weapon, Marshall fist-punched the air as he pulled himself up and into the aircraft. Positioning himself on the other side of the hold, he found his own minigun and checked it.

"Headsets!" Alvaradejo shouted as she pulled one on. The roar of the rotor blades slicing the air in half was deafening and quickly, the two men found their own and slipped them over their ears.

Smiling, Marshall said, "Let's get the fuck out of here!"

"What's that?" Dillahunt asked as they slowly rose off of the cement helipad.

Looking past him, Marshall saw the fast-moving flock of raptors charging the T-Rex. They streamed out of the jungle, shrieking and chirping at the wounded predator. It was quite a sight to see.

The wave of smaller dinosaurs barrelled into the larger dinosaur who snarled in anger before launching its own attack.

The massive head swung low, grazing the ground, scooping up the raptors in the opened jaws. Lifting itself up, the powerful jaws made short work of the trapped dinosaurs. Blood, flesh, and dismembered limbs fell from between the massive teeth.

"Just like Pendleton!" Dillahunt laughed as he rested his chin on the controls of the minigun. He smiled, happy with the show as Alvaradejo took them higher and higher.

Standing up, Marshall watched the prehistoric battle and had to admit it was one hell of a spectacle. But his mind tugged at him to ask Alvaradejo an important question. Tapping the speaker button, he said, "You know where we're going?"

Static crackled in his ears before he heard, "We've got GPS. I'll take us somewhere close, but safe. Don't worry, I'm not going to let anything happen to you *güeros*."

Laughing, Marshall didn't notice the shadow rise at them. By the time he turned and looked out his side of the helicopter, all he could scream was, "Pull up! There's another Rex!"

CHAPTER FIFTY-EIGHT

Alvaradejo heard the order just in time to pull up, then down on the joystick while working the pedals hard. The helicopter bucked from the sudden rough use, and she saw the massive jaws snap, closing around air.

"*¡Aguanta!*" she shouted a second before losing control of the helicopter. The aircraft went into a spin.

Figures, Marshall thought as he gripped the mounted gun. He felt the centripetal force compress him against the side of the hold.

Through the spinning, he could see the ocean whizz by. Then the helipad. The raptors battling the T-Rex and then the second Rex.

"Get this fucking under control!" he barked at the woman while fighting the urge to vomit. Though, if he did, the others wouldn't comment. The only thing that worried him was their proximity to the ground. If Alvaradejo couldn't get the helicopter under control and they crashed, then the only way out would be to use a boat, and he didn't want to risk getting caught by the waves.

"I'm doing it!"

"Walter! Start firing. We need to keep that thing off us!"

Not bothering to wait for confirmation, Marshall pressed the firing buttons on the gun's control. The multi-barrel cylinder spun, making an ear-piercing metallic grinding.

A second later, the tracer rounds spewed from the weapon.

It didn't matter what they hit. If it was the first T-Rex, then great. The raptors? Even better. For Marshall, he'd rather take out the newcomer. At least with one Rex, the raptors could deal with it. Two? That spelt certain disaster for them.

The helicopter stopped spinning; the sudden stop nearly hurled him against the wall. Instead, he held onto the minigun. The violent jerk swivelled it and the bullets took out a group of raptors.

A large, clawed, scaled foot crashed down in front of Marshall and he screamed, "Get us back up!"

On the other side of the helicopter, Dillahunt struggled with his own weapon. He couldn't see the new T-Rex, but the way the helicopter banked, then swooped up and down, it had to be there.

They were close enough to the ground that the faster dinosaurs had seen them and some were rushing towards them.

Mouths open and claws extended, it looked like they were ready to launch themselves at the Airbus H130.

"Pull up!" Dillahunt shouted, gritting his teeth.

"I'm doing it!" Alvaradejo's hands were slick with sweat, which made it harder to keep control of the aircraft.

Hearing the two bickering, Marshall quickly glanced behind him to see the charging dinosaurs. If they were lucky, the T-Rex would see them and step in the way. If not, then both would try for the prize, and he didn't know how much ammo he and Dillahunt had.

Chances were, it wouldn't be enough.

Looking back, he fired the mounted gun at the gaping maw of the T-Rex. The bullets thudded against its thick hide, riddling the soft tissue with bloody holes.

A shriek of pain came from the dinosaur, and it backed away.

Not wanting to give it another chance, Marshall pressed his attack and continued firing. The bullets couldn't penetrate the scaly flesh, but that didn't matter. He wanted to keep the animal at bay.

He stared at the head and a crazy idea formed.

With a grunt, he repositioned the minigun and stared down the barrel. The edge glowed bright red from the heat, and steam floated into the air. Ignoring the warning sign that it was overheating, he aimed for the most delicate parts of the T-Rex, then fired.

Blood erupted from the dinosaur's nostrils as the tracer rounds pierced the soft tissue. Shaking its head, the T-Rex tried to scratch at the wounds, but the stumpy arms couldn't reach.

Smiling at his success, Marshall continued firing, controlling the minigun with ease. The bullets moved from the nose to the ridges that protected the dinosaur's eyes.

Blood oozed from the wounds, but the eyes were clear of any damage.

"Incoming!"

Marshall turned, letting his gun go silent. Not thinking at all, he reached out and pulled Dillahunt away from the other minigun.

A raptor crashed into the side of the helicopter, impaling itself on the weapon, spewing blood all over the compartment. The legs, arms and jaws snapped and scratched at the two men as it bled out, dying slowly.

"Thanks, man," Dillahunt said a second before the T-Rex slammed its head into the helicopter.

CHAPTER FIFTY-NINE

Marshall crashed to the ground. His training kicked in and the moment he felt the impact, he rolled. Tucking his head against his chest, he heard the raptors chirp and purr before screaming at him.

Waiting for the perfect moment, he finished the roll and came up on his legs. *Oh shit!*

In front of him were the raptors. They stared at him, trying to figure out what to do. Behind them, he could see the first T-Rex. It was breathing hard and staggering about. In a few more minutes, it'd be dead.

The roar of the helicopter's blades mixed with the scream of a minigun made it clear that Alvaradejo and Dillahunt were still about and keeping the other Rex busy.

What now? Marshall thought, backing away from the animals. He knew they wouldn't wait before swarming him. It didn't matter as long as he could hold them back somehow. And thankfully, he still had the HK416.

Reaching down for it, his hand gripped thin air and fresh sweat bubbled to the surface of his face.

Where the fuck was it?

He risked a look and laughed. Sure enough, the rifle was gone. He still had the Tokarev TT-33 handgun. Though with that, he only had a couple of shots left. It wouldn't be enough to take out the dinosaurs.

A gust of wind broke his train of thought, and he looked up.

The helicopter was hovering above him. Dillahunt still worked the minigun while he kicked something out the side.

A metallic ladder unfurled, rolling until it came to a stop, fluttering in the wind.

"Fuck yeah!" Marshall shouted as he turned and ran. His right hand gripped the handgun and his legs burned with the desire to get off the island.

Behind him, the raptors bellowed their anger at the fleeing meal and gave chase. Their powerful legs propelled them faster than Marshall's and they closed the distance quickly. Like before, they lowered their heads, making them streamlined while their arms reached out, ready to tear into his skin.

A barrage of bullets kicked the dirt up behind Marshall, who sped up.

He had to make it to the swinging ladder.

The only problem was the heavy footsteps coming from the side.

Turning to the left, he saw the T-Rex jogging towards him. Its massive heavy feet crushed everything and the man knew he wouldn't make it in time.

So did Alvaradejo. She waved at him, then lifted the aircraft up and away. As they moved towards the sea, Marshall saw Dillahunt shouting something at her and pointing.

No hard feelings, he thought as a calm washed over him. He understood why she'd done it. Sacrifice one for the greater good and if push came to shove, he'd have done the same thing.

But it didn't mean he'd give up that easily.

Turning back, he raised the Tokarev and squeezed the trigger.

A raptor squealed before shaking its head. Blood dribbled from the wound on its neck and the animal slowed before collapsing.

"Fuck you!" Marshall shouted as he turned and saw the ocean. He could still escape!

It was a one in a million shot. If he dove off of the dock, he could swim out far enough and maybe float until he was rescued.

Fat chance, he thought, but it was better than nothing.

Tossing the now empty gun away, he took a deep breath and sped up.

His lungs burned from the exertion and darkness crept around the edges of his vision, but Marshall pushed himself harder and harder. If he could get past the physical pain and discomfort, he'd hit his reserves and be unstoppable.

But that was easier said than done.

He felt the sting of a blade across his back and fell. He rolled for a few metres. Pain exploded across his back and he knew one of the raptors had cut him.

Keep going!

The command sounded in his mind and he scrambled to his feet as another of the dinosaurs slipped on his blood and tumbled. Marshall laughed at the sight, then started running.

Looking at the pier, he figured he had twenty metres at most and then it would be the cold, wet embrace of the ocean. Seeing it, he felt energised. This was his only chance, and he hoped the dinosaurs couldn't swim or, at least, float.

The moment he felt the wooden slats under his feet, the creaking of the damp wood, Marshall started wooing like a drunken fool. It was the only sound he could make and as he leapt from the pier, his last words were, "I fucking hate dinosaurs!"

CHAPTER SIXTY

His entire body ached and Marshall cried out in pain. It would take months for him to get back to the physical condition he was in before the hunt. But the fact that he was feeling anything at all made Marshall open his eyes and smile.

He was back in the helicopter. The pattern of the roof was easy to remember and he could smell the aviation fuel and spent gunpowder. They had saved him!

Sitting up, Marshall groaned and reached for his head. At the same time, his back spasmed, making him whimper. Reaching behind him, he felt something wet and warm ooze from the wound, then dribble towards his ass.

"Stay, Seamus," Dillahunt said, gently pushing him back down. "We don't have the proper equipment to stitch up your back. Luckily, you're a heavy fucker, so the weight alone will stem the blood. For now."

Marshall managed a smile. "How?"

Before answering, the man slipped a headset onto Marshall's head, then tapped the microphone. "Say that again, Seamus."

"How?"

Dillahunt's smile grew bigger, and he puffed out his chest with pride. "I won. Freddie wanted to just fly away. Leave you to die. But when I saw you dive into the ocean, well, we just had to come back and make sure you weren't dead."

Rolling his head to the side, Marshall stared at the woman. Alvaradejo was focused on piloting.

"We're about ninety-minutes from Mexico. I've radioed ahead, and we'll have fresh clothes and doctors waiting for us. You're welcome," she said, turning to look at the man.

Before Marshall could speak, he coughed from the pain. His body spasmed, and he felt like his head was going to fall off. How much damage had he actually sustained? Or did something else happen once he dove into the water?

Dillahunt pursed his lips, then said, "We found you clinging to some rocks. Looks like you got bashed against them a couple of times. Rough waters. What the fuck did you think was going to happen?"

The only thing Marshall could do was shrug, groan, then fight the urge to pass out.

"Rest."

He shook his head. There was something he had to see. Opening his eyes, he stared at the other man and said, "I want to see it."

A look of concern washed over Dillahunt's face. He looked at the woman, who shrugged.

"Please." Marshall's voice was barely above a whisper, and he needed to make sure of something.

Nodding, Dillahunt helped him sit up and pointed to the small window in the side door.

Staring out of it, Marshall saw the fading shape of the island. He was truly off it and travelling back home. To freedom. To his life and future.

With a nod, he slid back to his original position and chuckled. Now he could rest. Sleep until the doctors patched him up and then he'd make his own way back to England and the service. He knew he'd have to go through rigorous testing and training again. Nobody got in that easily. But it would be worth it.

Then, after a couple months of active duty and working my way up again, Sean Marshall thought as darkness enveloped him, *I'll tell them about this place and then we'll do what we do best.*

THE END

ACKNOWLEDGEMENTS

None of this would be possible if it weren't for my parents. They have always supported me and helped me to reach my dreams. Thanks also needs to go to J.H. Moncrieff and Wes Parker you amazing authors have helped me so much. A special thanks needs to go to Diana Khasanova for helping me with research and translation. Also, thanks must go to the Australasian Horror Writer's Association and, of course, the amazing people at Severed Press, who without, this book wouldn't exist!

ABOUT THE AUTHOR

R.F. Blackstone has been writing for over 15 years, starting in the hallowed world of scripting. After many would-be deals with the Devil, R.F. decided to say "Screw it" then picked up the mantle of novelist and he has never looked back. His published works include *The Wild Hunt*, *Megaflora* and *The Valley of Bicho* for Severed Press and *Zombie Nazis On A Train* for D&T Publishing.

You can reach R.F. Blackstone at:
Facebook - https://www.facebook.com/Blackstone.RF
Twitter - https://twitter.com/RF_Blackstone
Instagram - https://www.instagram.com/rfblackstone/

Check out other great

Dinosaur Thrillers!

Steve Metcalf

OBJEKT 221

Ruthless multi-national conglomerate Allied Genetics is unde siege from a paramilitary force for hire. Allied calls i reinforcements and fortifies their crown-jewel property – a abandoned Soviet military facility in Crimea known during th Cold War as Objekt 221. Fortunately for the future of the research, O221 straddles a stretch of rocky landscape tha hides a rift – a portal through time and space. Through th rift, Allied Genetics can travel, at will, to the Cretaceous – 10 million years into Earth's past – and bolster their geneti experiments with dinosaur DNA ... something the competitors want to stop at all costs."Objekt 221" is a stor blending numerous science fiction elements such a repurposed military facilities, time travel, rogue corporat armies, dinosaurs and the hint of a super-ancient civilizatio

Bestselling collection

PREHISTORIC: A DINOSAUR ANTHOLOGY

PREHISTORIC is an action packed collection of storie featuring terrifying creatures that once ruled the Earth. Los worlds where T-Rex and Velociraptors still roam and ma is now on the menu. Laboratories at the forefront of clonin technology experiment with dinosaurs they do no understand or are able to contain. The deepest parts of th ocean where Megalodon, the largest and most ferociou predator to have ever existed is stalking new prey. Plu many more thrillers filled with extinct prehistoric monster written by some of the best creature feature authors th side of the Jurassic period.

check out other great

Dinosaur Thrillers!

Doug Goodman

HUNTING WITH DINOSAURS

A hunting party is sent to catch and kill raptors that have escaped Dinosaur Falls Restricted Area and murdered nearby hikers. But the hunters find the raptors are unlike any creature they've ever hunted, and soon one lone bowhunter is running for his life through the Perdidos Mountains. He discovers an old wilderness survival trench and burrows in deep, but eventually the raptors come for him. His only salvation is to befriend a wo f hellbent on destroying the raptors. If they can come together, they can form a pack the world has never seen, but if they fail, the raptors are waiting with their sharp teeth and elongated claws...

Edward J. McFadden III

DINOSAUR RED

There's a doorway on Mars that has mankind's greatest minds perplexed. Deep beneath Aeolis Mons an ancient secret is revealed, and a team of explorers led by Forest Judge, Deputy Commander of Gale Base Alpha, are dispatched to investigate. The prehistoric gateway reveals a biosphere preserving Earth's distant past, and as Judge and crew stand on the threshold of mankind's greatest discovery the Martian ground trembles. A roar thunders from within, the doorway closes, and the team is trapped. Six mission specialists, each with unique skills, each with different reasons for wanting to break free of the primordial trap. To get home Judge is forced to choose between escape and changing the course of humanity. What will he do?

Check out other great

Dinosaur Thrillers!

Greig Beck

PRIMORDIA: IN SEARCH OF THE LOST WORLD

Ben Cartwright, former soldier, home to mourn the loss of h
father stumbles upon cryptic letters from the past betwee
the author, Arthur Conan Doyle and his great, gre
grandfather who vanished while exploring the Amazon jung
in 1908. Amazingly, these letters lead Ben to believe that h
ancestor's expedition was the basis for Doyle's fantastic
tale of a lost world inhabited by long extinct creatures. A
Ben digs some more he finds clues to the whereabouts of
lost notebook that might contain a map to a place that is hom
to creatures that would rewrite everything known abou
history, biology and evolution. But other parties now kno
about the notebook, and will do anything to obtain it. For Be
and his friends, it becomes a race against time and again
ruthless rivals. In the remotest corners of Venezuela, alor
winding river trails known only to lost tribes, and through ne
impenetrable jungle, Ben and his novice team find a forbidde
place more terrifying and dangerous than anything they cou
ever have imagined.

William Meikle

THE LOST VALLEY

A remote high valley in the Canadian Rockies hides a
ecosystem that has been lost in time. A small team
prospectors and their local guides are looking for gold. Wh
they find is blood and terror and death.The valley's monstrou
inhabitants are not about to let go of its secrets lightly.

www.ingramcontent.com/pod-product-compliance
Lightning Source LLC
Chambersburg PA
CBHW061233170626
46809CB00007B/2649